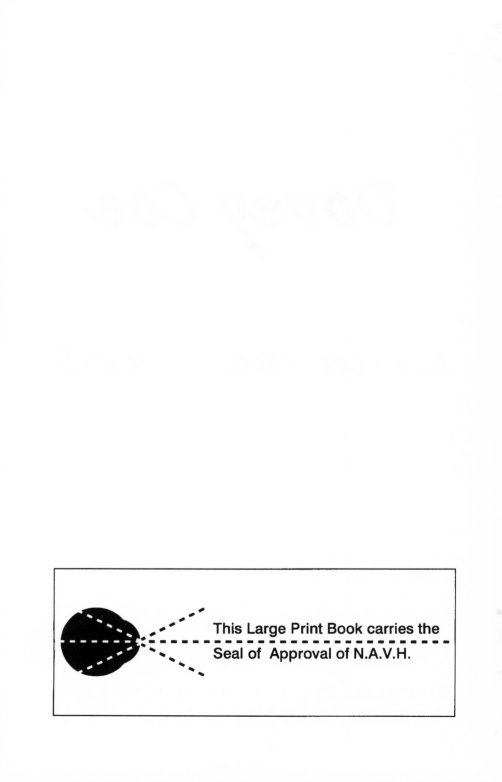

This Large Print Book carries the
Seal of Approval of N.A.V.H.

Dovey Coe

Frances O'Roark Dowell

Thorndike Press • Waterville, Maine

Published in 2001 by arrangement with
Simon & Schuster's Children's Publishing Division.

Thorndike Press Large Print Juvenile Series.

The tree indicium is a trademark of Thorndike Press.

The text of this Large Print edition is unabridged.
Other aspects of the book may vary from the original edition.

Set in 16 pt. Plantin by Al Chase.

Printed in the United States on permanent paper.

Library of Congress Cataloging-in-Publication Data
Dowell, Frances O'Roark.
    Dovey Coe / Frances O'Roark Dowell.
       p. cm.
    Summary: When accused of murder in her North Carolina
mountain town in 1928, Dovey Coe, a strong-willed
twelve-year-old girl, comes to a new understanding of others,
including her deaf brother.
    ISBN 0-7862-3590-X (lg. print : hc : alk. paper)
    1. Large type books. [1. Brothers and sisters — Fiction.
2. Mountain life — North Carolina — Fiction. 3. North
Carolina — Fiction. 4. Death — Fiction. 5. Murder —
Fiction. 6. Physically handicapped — Fiction. 7. Large type
books.] I. Title.
PZ7.D75455 Do 2001
[Fic]—dc21   2001041504

For Clifton and Jack

chapter 1

My name is Dovey Coe, and I reckon it don't matter if you like me or not. I'm here to lay the record straight, to let you know them folks saying I done a terrible thing are liars. I aim to prove it, too. I hated Parnell Caraway as much as the next person, but I didn't kill him.

I know plenty of folks who thought about it once or twice, after Parnell shot a BB gun at their cats or broke their daughters' hearts. They're the same ones who go around now making out like Parnell was an angel, a regular pillar of society. The truth is, there ain't no one in Indian Creek who didn't believe Parnell Caraway was the meanest, vainest, greediest man who ever lived. Seventeen years old and rotten to the core.

Of course, his daddy being the richest man in town meant Parnell could do about whatever he pleased without anybody saying *boo* back to him. Most of the folks who live in town rent their houses from Homer Caraway and buy their dry goods from his store, and they know better than to cross him. You so much as look at Homer Caraway wrong and he can make your life right miserable.

Every time I start complaining about having to walk a half mile down the mountain to school every morning, I remember how lucky we are to own our land. It ain't much — four acres, a five-room house, and a barn — but it keeps us Coes from being beholden to Homer Caraway, and I'd walk ten miles to school to keep it that way.

I know it pained Parnell that we weren't indebted to his daddy. Maybe if we had been, my sister Caroline would have married him the way he kept asking her to do. Caroline Coe was the one thing Parnell wanted he couldn't have. As conceited as Parnell was, it took him a long time to figure that out.

But I'm getting ahead of myself, which I do from time to time. You probably want to know where I'm from and who my family is, the particulars folks tend to be interested in.

Like I said, my name is Dovey Coe. There have been Coes living in Indian Creek, North Carolina, since the beginning of time, and I expect there always will be. We're mountain folk, and once you been living in the mountains for a while, it's hard to live anywhere else. You can walk over to the graveyard behind the church in town and see Coes going as far back as 1844. The most recent stone belongs to my Granddaddy Caleb, who passed on two years ago, when I was ten. It says: HERE LIES CALEB COE, LOVING HUSBAND TO REBECCA COE, FATHER TO MATTHEW, LUKE, AND JOHN COE. BORN MAY 17, 1861. DIED DECEMBER 2, 1926. MAY HE WALK WITH THE LORD.

John Coe is my daddy. He's what they call a jack-of-all-trades, meaning he can fix anything you got that's broke and some things that ain't. Folks bring him their busted radios, their haywire toasters, their broke-down automobiles, and Daddy tightens a screw here, reconnects a wire there, and makes it good as new. Them who have money to pay give him a dollar or two, depending on the size of the job, and them who don't have a dime in their pocket work out a barter. When Gaither Sparks's carburetor died, we got a new pig and a pound of sugar. It evens out, as Daddy is all the time saying.

Mama grew up over in Cane Creek Holler, not two miles from here. She still hums the songs she learned when she was a little girl while she works around the house, and she has taught many of them songs to me. I try my best to remember them the right way, and I always pretend like I'm paying attention when she's telling me all the things she says a young lady ought to know.

Besides Caroline, I got me an older brother named Amos, age of thirteen, and he loves good adventure as much as I do. We spend a good portion of our days running around on Katie's Knob, hunting arrowheads or hunks of crystal quartz, tracking all manner of wild animals and generally having a big time.

We live in the house my daddy grew up in, and every morning I look out upon the same mountains my daddy looked out upon when he was a child. I like sitting on the porch watching the summer evenings fall across the valley, listening to Daddy pick old tunes on his guitar. I enjoy the cozy feel of sitting next to the woodstove when there's a frosty bite in the air.

There's at least a million other things that all add up to my good life here, more things than I can say or even remember, they're so natural to me now.

That's why it's hard to believe they might send me away from here.

It's not that I blamed Caroline for this whole mess. I know deep inside it ain't exactly her fault. But on top of things, it sure feels that way.

chapter 2

"I reckon Parnell Caraway would do anything for you, including lay down and die," I said to Caroline one afternoon back in early summer, when Mama's garden was starting to push out every sort of vegetable known to mankind and it seemed like all we did was one chore after the other. Parnell was on my mind that morning, as I had been thinking about how rich folks like him and his sister, Paris, probably never had to do a single chore in their lives.

We was sitting in the shade of the front porch shelling peas for supper. I had finished shelling the peas in my basket and was starting on Caroline's, which was still half full. Caroline was always making plans in her head, and doing something so ordinary as shelling peas didn't make much of a claim on her attention.

"Good Lord, Dovey," Caroline said, sounding like I was too addle-brained to be listened to. "Parnell don't care no more for me than he cares for a chicken."

She ran a hand through her dark hair, her cheeks reddening. From the look in her eyes, I'd say she right enjoyed the idea of some boy laying down and dying for her, not that she'd admit it.

Caroline was sixteen, a whole four years older than myself, but a lot of folks said I acted like the older sister because I weren't afraid of anything and I'd speak my mind when it was called for. They sure didn't mistake me for the prettier sister.

She was so pretty, sometimes I could hardly look at her. It was like she had a white light around her setting off her long dark hair and big green eyes. Daddy said Caroline could stop an army of men with them eyes of hers, and I believed it. I have gray eyes myself, and there ain't enough about them to comment upon.

"I reckon Parnell is low-down enough to love a chicken," I teased her, wanting to stay in her good graces. There was no fun to be had when Caroline fell into one of them moods of hers.

My chicken remark got her to laughing. "Ain't you something," she said, swatting my knee, "going on that way about chickens and love."

Caroline stood up, brushing peas from her green cotton skirt, and went into the house. I would have bet you one dollar right then and there she was going to go lie across the bed and dream her big dreams about leaving for faraway places without giving a second thought to Parnell Caraway, even though he had been trying to get her to spend time with him for nearly a year.

You see, by the time Caroline had turned fourteen, she had come up with a plan for her life, having decided that living here in Indian Creek was not for her. She wanted to get herself a taste of the world and see what lay beyond these mountains. So she decided she would go to teachers college over in Boone.

She figured that when she finished she'd be able to get a good teaching job in Asheville or maybe even down in Charlotte or Raleigh, and send a little money home to Mama and Daddy. The rest she would spend on pretty clothes and weekend trips to interesting spots. For a long time, Parnell's attentions didn't seem to affect her in the least bit.

I sat finishing up the peas Caroline had left, looking out over the yard and into the woods beyond. To my way of thinking, if you was born a Coe, then Indian Creek was where you belonged. Coes had lived in this town going on forever, and we were as much a part of it as Katie's Knob and Cane Creek. But as usual Caroline had figured things differently from the way I did.

I wondered some about what it would be like to be Caroline, to have boys coming at you this way and that, their hearts in their hands. Not that I was all that interested in boys, mind you. Nor did I wish to be some raving beauty, since my interests did not lie in the area of romance. Just sometimes I got curious, is all.

One morning Caroline woke me up right early, holding a mug of hot chocolate under my nose, a guaranteed way to get me up of a morning, as Caroline known better than most.

"Dovey, honey, let's go into town and see what they've got at the farmers market." Caroline give me a smile that said, *please, oh, please*. It had an effect on me, and I jumped right up and started pulling on my dungarees and blouse.

It was a bright Saturday morning, and as usual Caroline was half afraid to go down the mountain by herself. All sorts of wild animals lived in these mountains; we could hear them talking to each other at night, and it was enough to scare a person sitting on the safety of their porch. During the day, though, it was real rare to see a bear or a cougar. I weren't bothered by the thought of roaming through the woods by myself or with Amos to look for the roots we sold to doctors who lived off the mountain. But Caroline was another story. She was sure she was going to get eaten by a mountain lion unless I was there to beat it off with a stick.

By the time we got to town, Caroline had forgotten all about the wild things. Her mind was on the market and what she might find there. Starting in the spring, farmers brought their families to town and set up a market at the end of King Street, which was the street that run through the middle of things. They sold a variety of goods, not just their produce. You'd see tables set up to sell breads and cakes, quilts of every pattern — Water Wheel, Goose Wing, and Dove in the Window — wooden ducks and pups you could pull along with a string, jars full of marbles, jars full of buttons, an old spinning wheel or a quilting frame that had been gathering dust in somebody's barn, just every sort of thing, and every once in a while you'd run into a veritable treasure.

Caroline and I ambled through the farmers market, enjoying the good smells and the sight of the many fine things we would buy if we had the money. We stopped in front of a table that held among its fineries a silver-plated mirror and a steel-blade, shiny, red-cased pocketknife. I'd been wanting a pocketknife since the first time I seen one in the Sears and Roebuck catalog. There it sat in the picture, shiny and a little dangerous looking, though I didn't point out that aspect of it to Mama. I could think of a hundred ways of using it, from hacking weeds in the garden to defending myself against a cougar if I ever come across one.

I tried to get Mama interested in the idea of getting me that pocketknife for Christmas, but she weren't having none of it. Mama was trying to wean me from my more boyish ways. "It ain't ladylike to cross your legs that way," she'd tell me, or, "I'm going to make you give me a nickel for every time I see you spitting in the yard." I'd see her frown at me from the porch when I set out to go fishing with Amos at the pond out back, and she was all the time telling Daddy I was getting too old to help him fix up cars in the barn.

Caroline kept picking up the mirror and turning it in her hand, trying not to admire her reflection in it too much. Me, I was busy testing the weight of the pocketknife in my hand. It felt just right. The only problem was it cost fifty cents, and I only had a nickel.

A boy who looked to be about sixteen, with spotty skin and an Adam's apple you couldn't help but stare at, stood behind the table and kept his eyes glued to Caroline. Anybody could tell he thought he'd died and gone to heaven from the way his mouth fell half open, a slack smile curling up the corner of his lips.

"That there's a pretty mirror for a real pretty girl, if you don't mind me saying so," is what he finally managed to say, pointing a bony finger at his table and looking right proud that he'd gotten that much out of his mouth.

Caroline aimed them green eyes of hers directly at him and laughed that laugh of hers that hits you like a cool drink of water on an August afternoon. "Well, ain't you so sweet to say that? I was thinking how fine this would look on my dresser at home."

The boy begun to look a little peaked, like he was thinking of Caroline sitting in her nightgown in front of her dresser table. He swallowed a few times, that Adam's apple bobbing up and down in a way that was right fascinating.

"It's too bad it's so costly," Caroline went on, swaying her hips a bit like she were dancing to a song only she could hear, weaving her spell. "I just don't have two dollars to spend."

"Well, my mama might have my hide, but I'll tell you what. I'll let you have it for one dollar even, just because you're so pretty."

Caroline shook her head sweetly. "You are the nicest thing. Most boys as handsome as you ain't half so nice."

I was getting a little bored with all the pleasantries going back and forth between the two of them. I started humming a loud tune and bumping into Caroline's side with my hip.

"This is my little sister, Dovey," Caroline said, introducing me to the boy, who give me a quick nod before getting back to the business of my sister. "She sure does seem to fancy that pocketknife."

I had lost all patience with their little courtship. "Come on, Caroline, let's go. You ain't got the money for the mirror, I ain't got the money for the pocketknife, and Mama wants us home in time for dinner."

Caroline looked sorrowfully at her would-be suitor and said, "I guess Dovey's right, we really should be going."

Before you could say *Davy Crockett*, the boy asked me, "How much money you got?"

"I got one U.S. nickel, and that ain't enough to buy anything you're selling."

"Don't be so sure." Before you know it, he'd wrapped the mirror and the pocketknife in brown paper and said, "That will be five cents, please, and could I interest you pretty ladies in a lemonade, my treat?"

When Mama saw my pocketknife that afternoon, she put up a fuss, but Daddy convinced her that a girl who spends as much time on the mountain as I do needs a good knife. He was a touch curious about how me and Caroline had gotten such a fine bargain on our purchases, but we just left that topic alone, and soon enough Daddy got to thinking on other matters.

Sometimes I weren't sure that it was right for Caroline to act the way she did with men, getting them to do every little thing for her, especially since she could get real sensitive about people thinking that she weren't nothing more than a pretty face. But if ever I started to judging her too harshly, I just took out that knife and remembered that she weren't the only one who profited from her ways.

"You just be careful with that thing, Dovey," Mama told me as I was fixing to go out the door after dinner. Me and Amos was

20

going to check some of our traps up on Katie's Knob. "I'm good with a needle, but I don't know how to sew fingers back on to a hand."

Caroline was sitting at the kitchen table polishing up her silver mirror with a dish towel. "Try not to kill anyone with that thing, Dovey," she warned me in a joking manner. "I'd sure hate to have to come bail you out of jail."

"Caroline, where on earth do you get the notion to say such a thing?" Mama scolded. Mama was real sensitive about bloodshed and violence. Her youngest brother, Cecil, had been shot and killed in the fields of Argonne, France, in the Great War, and Mama still hadn't got over that.

"Oh, Mama," Caroline said, sounding like she weren't taking Mama the least bit seriously. Then she started humming some song I'd never heard before. The music of her voice trailed me out the door and up the mountain path.

chapter 3

Amos had gotten way ahead of me by the time I got out the door. He known every rock, every gopher hole, every twist of the dirt path that wound up Katie's Knob to all the good and secret places that the mountain held, and he could move along it like a slip of wind. I had trekked that path many a time myself, but Mama's hand was always reaching out to pull me back into the life of proper things and tiny stitches and delicate sighs. Amos was older than me by a year, and he was allowed to roam freely, so that he known that mountain like he known his own face in the mirror.

When I finally caught up with him, he was kneeling down to examine some animal tracks that veered from the path off into the woods. Tom and Huck, Amos's dogs, had already burrowed through a thick growth of vines and weeds to follow the scent of whichever creature had been there. I figured it to be a deer by the V of the track, and when I said this to Amos, he nodded and rose. We had no interest in deer this time of year. It was roots and herbs we could sell for medicinals that we had an eye peeled for.

Amos clapped out his signal for Tom and Huck, and the dogs come running back to us. Their yellow fur was full of burrs and spotted with red clay, and they was panting from what seemed to me to be the sheer joy of the chase.

I don't know if I can even explain what a comfort them dogs were to me. I had made Amos my responsibility from the time we were little ones, but after Mama started her campaign to make a lady out of me, I couldn't always keep him in my sights. I pointed this out to her again and again, but she weren't having none of it. "Amos can get along by his own self, Dovey," she'd lecture me. "Let him grow up some." But not once had Mama bloodied her knuckles on some fool of a boy who'd come up behind Amos and made crazy faces, whereas I bore many a scar.

Here's the truth of the matter: When Amos was born, he could hear as good as you or me. What happened, they say, is that he got a sickness when he was still little, and it caused water to be in his head and make his brain swell, and because of it he turned deaf. Mama started suspecting something was wrong when Amos were about ten months old. She'd walk into her room where Amos laid in his crib, and he wouldn't give any sign he known she was there until she stood right in front of him. She'd clap her hands from behind him, but he didn't take no notice. Finally she and Daddy took him to the doctors over in Asheville, who said for sure Amos was deaf and wouldn't ever hear again.

Some folks thought that because Amos didn't hear and he didn't talk, he must be stupid, and a lot of folks treated him like he was, though it was a far sight from the truth. I taught Amos to read when he was eight and I was seven, which weren't as hard to do as you might think. I started him out with picture books that had just a few words. So there'd be a picture of a dog and the word "dog," and Amos made the connection right quick. If there was a word that didn't have a picture of it attached, I'd just find a real-life example and show it to him.

Later on, I taught him how to read lips in pretty much the same way, and soon he could understand just about anything a person would care to say to him as long as they spoke directly to his face. He couldn't talk, but he could write. In fact, his handwriting was a sight prettier than mine.

Mama said my writing looked like a chicken dipped in ink had walked across my paper.

Amos never went to school, for which I envied him greatly. The school in Indian Creek was a poor excuse for an institution of learning. Every year we got us some wet-behind-the-ears teacher straight out of teachers college who thought she was doing her Christian duty by coming up here and learning us hillbillies. I give them six months at most, and they tended not to last more than four. Partly it was because winter up here hit early and hard, sending flatlanders directly back to where they come from. The other part was that it appeared teachers college didn't teach you how to handle boys like Lonnie Matthews and Curtis Shrew, who made it their business to send wet-behind-the-ears teachers out of town on a rail.

As soon as the new teacher left, old Mrs. Dreama Bullock took the wheel. She was about as deaf as Amos and had the learning of a brick. The only way to gain any real learning in Indian Creek was to get books from the library, which Amos and I did every week. His favorite books were those by Mr. Mark Twain, which was how he come to name his dogs Tom and Huck. Come to think of it, Amos looked like how I imagined Huck Finn to look, real boyish with a face full of merriment.

When Amos and me would get back to the house from the library, he'd head straight for the kitchen, where he'd get himself a glass of milk, sit down at the table, and commence to reading. He wouldn't budge until Mama shooed him out so she could get supper fixed. He'd come looking for me then, and the two of us would play cards or dig in the yard for precious gems until it was time to eat. Sometimes we'd sit on Amos's bed and draw maps leading to a buried treasure, and then we'd search around Amos's room looking for something to bury out in the yard that we could dig up later. Amos might have had neat handwriting, but his room was a mess. You'd find everything in the world under his bed: birds' nests, twigs, colored pencils, little smooth stones from up on Cane Creek, feathers — it was all there.

I reckoned Amos was about the best friend I had. I had other friends here and there, of course. Wilson Brown was a boy my age at school who I was good friends with. He was tall and skinny and a bit on the quiet side, but he was always up for an adventure and knew a good bit about rocks and plant life. We'd always gotten along just fine, but he and I didn't have the closeness I had with Amos.

It's true there weren't nothing I wouldn't do for my brother, and I did as much as I could. I believe this was also true for Tom and Huck, who stayed by Amos at all times and wouldn't let no harm fall to him. We never worried about Amos roaming the mountain by himself, because Tom and Huck was always with him.

The wind begun to pick up some as we moved toward the peak of Katie's Knob, always checking right and then left for what might lurk in the trees and behind the rocks that here and there jutted up from the dirt like craggy teeth. On an afternoon such as this, cool for July, a breeze blowing, we was out for adventure as much as medicinals. Though it had been some time since Indians had walked this trail, I still wished we might see some, or that maybe we'd cross paths with a runaway from Virginia or Tennessee who we could build a shelter for and bring food to.

Amos held up his hand, motioning for me to stop in my tracks. I didn't see nothing in our path, but that didn't mean that there weren't nothing there. A bit of excitement tickled the back of my neck. Maybe Amos had noted a stranger off to the side of the trail, or maybe he had picked up the scent of a bear lumbering toward her den in the distance. I slid my hand into the pocket of my dungarees and felt of my knife in its red case, its metal edges cool against my fingers, and touched my thumbnail to the blade's groove so that I could flick it open quick if I needed to attack.

The pounding of wings filled the air like a burst of thunder. "Good Lord have mercy!" I yelled. The bird that rose in our path was a sight, its wings spreading so wide as to reach practically from one side of the trail to the other. Its beak was as long as a pencil and curved downward, and feathers stood straight up atop its head like a headdress worn by a Sioux chieftain. I had never seen such a thing up on Katie's Knob. I reckoned that bird must have gotten off track from its normal course, and I said as much to Amos when he turned to look at me, grinning from ear to ear.

He nodded, then turned and chased after the thing, Tom and Huck directly on his heels. I run behind them, shaking my head, wondering what on earth Amos would do if he happened to catch the bird. But the thought had barely made tracks across my mind before the bird got ahold of the air and headed for the sky and whatever distant land it called home.

We had reached the top of Katie's Knob by this time, and Indian Creek spread out below us like a quilt. Amos fell to the ground, breathing hard from the chase. Tom and Huck licked at his face and neck, which made Amos shake with laughter.

I sat down beside him, my breath short and quick. There was no use in trying to talk with Amos rolling around on the ground with Tom and Huck. From down the mountain I could hear the bell Mama rang to bring me in when I'd gone out past the yard and she needed me home to help her. By the look of the sun, I'd say it was close to suppertime. Lately, Mama had me setting the table every night with a full complement of forks and spoons and knives so that I would know the proper thing to do should I find myself in high society.

As far as I was concerned, where I sat was high society enough, there with my brother and the birds and every wild thing.

chapter 4

Sunday afternoon, two weeks later, Caroline pulled the ledger book from the kitchen drawer after church, sat down at the table to study on it, and commenced to crowing with delight.

"I knew it! All I could think about at church was how maybe when that sow got big enough for Daddy to sell it to Chester Daniels, we'd have enough for tuition, and I was right!"

Caroline's cheeks was flushed all red, and she had a big smile on her face. "I can't hardly believe it!" she said, throwing her head back and grinning at the ceiling. "I am finally going to get out of this town."

"Do us all a favor, honey," my mama said from where she was standing at the side-board, still dressed in her navy blue church dress with the pearl buttons, slicing a cold ham for dinner. "At least act like you're a little bit sad at the thought of going."

Caroline rose from her seat and walked over to Mama's side. "You know I'm going to miss everyone, Mama," she said, giving Mama a little squeeze around the shoulders. "But there is a world out there, and I aim to see it."

"You aim to see all the handsome gentlemen," I said. I had taken a seat on the floor where I could lean my back against the cold woodstove and thumb through a right interesting book about rock collecting.

Caroline give me a tight smile. "What I am talking about is getting an education," she said, trying to sound proper, as was her practice of late. "I do have a brain in my head, you know. It's important for someone of my talents and abilities to get cultivated. I hear that Boone is filled with cultivated folks. And Asheville, too."

"Bunch of jokers with their fingers sticking out when they drink their tea, I bet you," I told her, sounding just like my daddy.

"Now how on earth would you know a thing about tea drinking, Dovey?" Caroline questioned me. "You still haven't learned to wipe the milk off your lip after you take a swig."

I did not find that comment worthy of reply.

A lot of folks wondered why Caroline was taking the bother of going off to college, seeing as she was likely to get married before too long, a girl as pretty as she was. They didn't reckon on Caroline being the sort of girl whose head held a bigger picture than marrying as soon as she finished high school and moving in next door to her mama, which is what most of the girls in Indian Creek did. That weren't my aim, personally, nor had it ever been Caroline's. Us Coes were made of more interesting stuff than that.

My daddy sold that pig to Chester Daniels the following Monday, and then he rode over to Boone on Tuesday and paid down the money for Caroline to go to teachers college in the fall. By the time Wednesday morning rolled around, Coreen Lovett had cornered Mama in Caraway's Dry Goods, where Mama was buying flour to make a pound cake, and asked her if it was true about Caroline going off to college. It didn't take long for a piece of news to get around in Indian Creek, that was the honest truth.

"Folks in this town sure love to talk, don't they?" Mama said when she got back from Caraway's. "I reckon even Cypress Terrell and his mama have heard about Caroline's going to school by now."

Cypress Terrell was a little old feller without any teeth who lived with his mama up yonder on Cane Creek. You might have seen them once or twice a year, that's how much they cared for the society of other folks.

Now when Parnell Caraway heard that my daddy had gone and done such a thing, he got in his automobile and drove on up the hill to our house, which ain't easy to do in a fancy car. But Parnell was a determined man, and he would sacrifice his car's good looks to make things turn out his way.

If it weren't for Caroline, Parnell Caraway wouldn't even consider stepping foot on our property. None of them Caraways thought us Coes was much good, but Parnell made an exception for Caroline, seeing as he was in love with her and all. He'd come by from time to time, just to see if Caroline had changed her mind about him. Sometimes Caroline was right friendly to Parnell; other times she didn't give him the time of day. Frankly, I think Parnell right enjoyed the confusion. All the other girls in town let it be known they thought Parnell hung the moon, but Caroline kept things interesting.

When Tom and Huck heard the sound of the engine, they like to have gone crazy, barking their heads off and running to show Amos that we had some excitement coming our way. This weren't the first time Parnell come to call, but usually Amos had Tom and Huck with him up on the mountain, so Parnell was a fairly unusual occurrence to their way of thinking.

Daddy stuck his head out from the barn, where he was fixing Luther McDowell's tractor alternator, and gave Parnell a wave as he was getting out of the car. From the garden, I seen Parnell stride over to the barn, and him and Daddy had themselves a short chat. I was dying to know what they was talking about. That was always a problem with Daddy. He'd be friendly with about anybody who passed his way. I was concerned he might not know all there was to know about Parnell. Daddy might take a liking to Parnell without understanding Parnell's true character or the fact that Parnell's people thought they was so much above us.

Parnell shook Daddy's hand and headed up to where I was tending Mama's flower garden. He wore a real determined look on his face, which I hated to admit was handsomer than ever. I have never denied that Parnell was a good-looking boy, although I always thought his looks was ruined by a meanness in his eyes. He had shiny black hair he wore slicked back on his head all wavylike, and the most perfect nose I'd ever seen. Just as straight and fine as a nose could be. His eyes were of a deep dark brown, like a deer's, and his skin was pale and creamy. Parnell had grown full into a man by that time and stood about six foot tall. He was a sight muscle-bound for a person who never done a day's work in his life.

"Hey, Dovey," he said, paying no mind to Amos, who had followed Tom and Huck out to the garden to see what all their fuss was about. For folks like Parnell, the fact of Amos being deaf made him invisible to their eyes, no need to give him a wave of the hand or a hello.

"What's got you up here, Parnell?" I asked, standing and wiping the dirt from my hands.

"Well, howdy do to you, too. I come to have me a little talk with Caroline. She around the house?"

Parnell walked over to me like he aimed to pat me on the shoulder or be friendly in some manner, but I moved too quick for him to get close to me. Parnell weren't going to get to Caroline by acting sweet to me, if that was what he was thinking. I had seen Parnell in his daddy's store acting as though the world was his to buy and sell, and he was not going to get on my good side, no matter how hard he tried.

By this time, Tom and Huck was sniffing around at Parnell's feet and trying to stick their noses in the crotch of his cream-colored pants, the way dogs are wont to do. Parnell give Huck a sharp kick and swatted Tom away with his hand. Amos started toward him with his hoe.

"I reckon I'd treat them dogs a little more neighborly if I was you," I told Parnell. "Amos don't take kindly to folks beating on his dogs."

Parnell held up his hands in the air like he was surrendering and said real loud, "Sorry 'bout that, Amos. Them dogs of yours was making me nervous is all."

That's when Caroline come out to the porch, looking pretty as could be in a blue flowered dress and no shoes on her feet. "Mama wants to know what all the fuss is out here," she said. "Oh, hey, Parnell. I thought I heard someone drive up. What's got you up here on such a fine afternoon?"

Parnell's expression softened like butter, and his voice got kind of gentle and quivery, not at all like his usual tone. "Caroline, I have to talk to you. It's real important."

Caroline sat down on the steps. "Why,

whatever's the matter, Parnell? You sick? You look a little peaked."

Parnell glanced over at me and then lowered his voice. "I'm sick with the thought of you going away," Parnell said, and I thought I might just get sick myself. "They say you're leaving for teachers college come August, but I aim to change your mind."

Parnell give me and Amos a look that meant for us to hightail it on out of there. I smiled the sweetest smile I had in me and started picking weeds out of the garden again. Amos went to tend to his dogs in the yard.

Parnell sat down on the step below Caroline, better to gaze at her famous eyes, I supposed. He took one of her hands in his own, which made Caroline raise an eyebrow, but she didn't take back her hand the way I thought she should have.

"Caroline, stay in Indian Creek and I'll make you the happiest girl alive, I swear to it," Parnell said, his words all full of emotion. "I'll buy you whatever you want, all the dresses in the world, rings on all your fingers, a car, whatever you say."

This is where I thought Caroline ought to have said something about how she longed to see the world and meet upstanding young gentlemen, and had no interest in staying in

Indian Creek. Instead, what she said was, "Why, I don't even know how to drive, Parnell. What do I need a car for?"

"You're missing my point, Caroline," Parnell said, starting to sound the littlest bit irritated. "What I'm saying is, marry me. I'll take care of your folks. I'll even send Amos to one of them special schools for deaf children."

"Now wait one hellfire minute, Parnell Caraway!" I interrupted from where I stood in the garden. "You ain't sending Amos nowhere!"

"Dovey!" Caroline called in a firm voice. "Let me take care of this!"

"A girl such as yourself shouldn't be using language like that," Parnell added, sounding peevish.

"Damnation and hell!" I replied. "Why don't you take your sorry self back to your daddy's store?"

Caroline stood up. "Now both of you, hush! Dovey, go on inside now so I can talk to Parnell."

I let the screen door slam behind me so to show them I was none too pleased about being sent away like I was some little child. Then I went and sat by the open window in the parlor room, where I could hear every word that was said between the two of them.

"What do you say, Caroline?" Parnell asked. "Will you marry me? I promise to take real good care of you and your family."

Caroline was quiet for a moment, collecting her words. Here's where she's going to tell him about getting some culture and having new experiences, I thought. Here's where she's going to remind Parnell he don't mean a thing to her. I smiled to myself and waited for the blow to fall.

But, "I'm awful flattered, Parnell, truly I am," is what she said, and I had to keep myself from shouting out. "But this proposal, well, it come out of nowhere. We ain't even been courting."

"Shoot, we've known each other since we was little children," Parnell protested. "At least promise me you'll think on the matter. That's all I ask. Let me come call on you in a regular way. Will you at least do that?"

"I'll have to ask Daddy. But even if he says yes, and I don't know that he will, it don't mean I'm going to marry you."

"Just give me a chance, is all I ask. I reckon you'll see things my way come August."

"I'll see what Daddy says," Caroline told him. "I'll ask him tonight after supper."

"You won't regret it," come Parnell's reply.

I looked out the window and seen Parnell walking to his car, Amos holding on tight to Tom and Huck so they wouldn't chase after him. Even from behind, Parnell looked cocky and full of himself, and hateful as it is to say, I believe if I'd had a gun in my hand, I would've been tempted to shoot him then and there.

But not on that day, or any other, did I ever harm a hair on Parnell Caraway's head.

chapter 5

From the beginning there was no love lost between Parnell Caraway and me, not even in the early years, though as Parnell got older he tried to pretend like he got along with everyone. That right there was acting on a grand scale.

I remember the time that I was nine and had brought Amos down to Caraway's Dry Goods to pass the afternoon, maybe finger through a comic book or two and buy us some jawbreakers. I won't soon forget the sight of the electric train set Parnell's mama and daddy give him for Christmas spread out across the floor, the tracks curving around the barrels full of sugar and flour and making a straightaway down past the canned goods.

A pack of children had gathered around where Parnell was kneeling on the floor, running them little trains. Me and Amos joined them to take a gander. All of us was dying to help Parnell set up the miniature village that come with the trains, or even just once flip the switch to start them little cars up.

Parnell looked around the crowd, a big grin on his face, a lock of black hair falling over his forehead. "Y'all don't touch a thing, you hear?" he said, his voice friendly on the top of it with a little river of meanness flowing beneath. "Now maybe if you give me a dollar each, I might let you help out some, but otherwise, you're flat out of luck."

Of course there weren't no one who had a dollar to give. Parnell and Paris Caraway were the only children in Indian Creek who ever had much spending money. The rest of us had pockets full of jacks and marbles and the smooth stones you could find up by Cane Creek, but not a dollar bill to save our lives. And Parnell known it, too.

"You let me play with your trains, I'll help you clean up when you're done," I said, coming up with the idea on the spot and thinking it a fair offer.

Parnell laughed. "Didn't know you was a cleaning lady, Dovey Coe. I'll tell my daddy for the next time he's looking to hire someone to sweep up in here."

I looked Parnell straight in the eye. "You're a sorry one, Parnell. I ain't offering to be your maid, I just want to mess with them trains."

"Too bad they ain't your trains, now ain't that right?" Parnell said, the grin still spread across his face. Then he turned back to the track, flipping the switches all by himself, them children just staring with their mouths open, dying for the teeniest chance to play. Amos got so frustrated, he kicked the side of the soda cooler a couple of times.

"Ain't y'all trained that little monkey yet?" Parnell had asked without even looking up from his trains. "Or is he too stupid to be made civilized?"

I grabbed Amos's hand and pulled him out of there before I gave in to my deep desire to aim a can of peas straight for Parnell's head.

Remembering just how evil Parnell could be, I was right scared that Caroline might lose her senses and take the boy up on his offer of marriage. There was more than a couple reasons the prospect bothered me, the least of which was that I couldn't stand the thought of being related to Parnell, even if it was just by law. But more than that to me was the worry he'd take a notion to send Amos away. I decided I had better have a talk with Daddy, especially after he done told Caroline that Parnell could call on her regular, if that's what she wanted.

It was warm that night, the breeze floating

real gentle over everything, like it were a mama putting her babies to sleep. Daddy was out on the porch with his guitar, picking one of them songs that about makes you want to cry even if you were right happy before you heard it. I waited for Daddy to finish his picking before I commenced to speak.

"Daddy, I ain't so sure about this business of Parnell calling on Caroline," I said flat out, the way I'm like to do.

Daddy strummed a few chords. "Now, why might that be, Sister?"

"You know how Parnell is, Daddy. He's bad news for everyone concerned."

"I admit it can take a while for Parnell to grow on a man," Daddy said, measuring out his words slow the way he did whenever he was giving some thought to a topic. "But this ain't got to do with my feelings on the matter. Caroline's just about a grown woman now, and I reckon it's up to her who she passes an evening with. When you turn sixteen, I won't tell you your business, either."

"But, Daddy," I said, a little panic creeping into me, "what if she goes and marries Parnell?"

Daddy laughed. "Then I reckon we'll start having Sunday dinner with Homer and

44

Lucy Caraway. That's a good way for a man to lose his appetite, now ain't it?"

"I'm serious, Daddy."

Daddy took a long look at me. "By your face, it appears you are. Well, tell me this, Sister. How likely you think it is that Caroline will break down and marry old Parnell? He's been coming around here on and off for a full year now, and she ain't never took much notice of him before. I reckon she's just passing the time."

"I know what you're saying is true," I told him, leaning forward in my chair. "But I've thought a right long time on this matter, and I can see how she might go and take Parnell up on his proposal. You see, Caroline might start to thinking if she married Parnell, then he'd give us all the money and things we needed. She'd think she was doing us a favor."

"What makes you think Parnell would give us anything?" Daddy asked, the least bit of an edge to his voice.

"He promised Caroline he would. I heard him. And, Daddy, if Parnell was giving us money all of the time, he'd figure he could be the boss of us, and he'd send Amos off to one of them homes where we'd never see him again."

Daddy set his guitar against the chair next

to him. Then he looked at me real hard, like he didn't much like what he was seeing. "I expect you best think real careful about what you're saying, Sister."

"All I'm saying, Daddy, is that Parnell —"

Daddy cut me off. "All you're saying is I'm a man who can be bought by the likes of Parnell Caraway. All you're saying is I'd let another man do what he pleased with my children. Is that what you think of me, Sister?"

I was right at the edge of tears. "No, Daddy, I don't think that way at all!"

Daddy picked up his guitar. "Get on out of here, Sister. I don't think I want your company right now." He started picking at some notes, not paying me any mind, even though I sat where I was for a couple of minutes before going up to my room, the tears running on down my face. It was like I had been made invisible to him.

Well, I can tell you I felt like the worst person that ever lived. The more I thought on it, the more I could see the error of my ways. Being so worried about what Parnell might do if he got ahold of Amos, I done neglected to consider that Daddy might have some say in the matter. Us Coes are proud people, but I'd gone and let that fact slip right out of my head. I admit that's my biggest drawback, not thinking things through far enough.

The next day Daddy weren't no friendlier than he had been the night before. He didn't so much as look at me over breakfast. Amos was fixing to take Tom and Huck up to the mountain to lay out traps for rabbits, and I decided to go along. Maybe if I got out of Daddy's way for a while, he'd get to missing me and act more kindly next time he saw me.

Me and Amos gathered up some traps from the barn and took off for the mountain, Tom and Huck right on our heels. Even though the path can be steep in places, usually I don't take no notice of it. I can climb right far up without having to stop to catch my breath. But on this particular day, I felt like I had a bag of stones strapped to my back. It weren't the traps that were so heavy, it was my bad feelings about what I had said to Daddy.

Katie's Knob ain't the tallest mountain in these parts, but it's close to it. You can see it from right far away. It's mostly pines growing up there, and that smell is as cool and fresh as any you're likely to come across. If I'm having a particular bad day, I like to go sit in a soft bed of pine needles be-

47

neath one of them trees and just breathe in real deep till I come back to my regular self.

It weren't unusual for Amos to get ahead of me when we was walking up to the peak. He was right quick, and when he had a plan in mind, he tended to get straight on it. I was more likely to take my time and keep an eye out for tracks in case there was a cougar about. That afternoon, though, Amos let Tom and Huck run on ahead while he stayed at my side. He didn't have no idea about what had occurred between me and Daddy, but it was like he known how low I was feeling. Amos didn't go in for much hugging the way he did when he was littler, but on that day he'd take my hand from time to time and give it a little squeeze, which was a great comfort to me.

Mama was sitting at the kitchen table when we come off the mountain, writing in her little book. Mama liked to keep notes on things, such as what Pastor Bean preached about on Sunday or the first day of spring that the flowers showed their blooms. Daddy said she was a historian, and years from now her grandbabies and great-grandbabies would be able to know how things were in the old days without having to go to the library to study on it.

The kitchen was bright with sunshine,

yellow rays streaming through the curtains and settling over everything, giving the room a clean, soft feeling. Amos went off to his room to tie some fishing flies for an afternoon out back by the pond, and I sat down across from Mama, hoping she might have some advice for me on how to get back in Daddy's favor.

Mama closed her book and set down her pencil. "You'uns get them traps set?" she asked, her eyes holding a more serious concern.

"Yes'm," I answered, rolling a grain of salt across the table with my finger. "I reckon we'll get us one or two rabbits at least. We might get some money for their furs to help with Caroline's schooling. That is, if she still aims to go on to teachers college."

"That weighs on your mind real heavy, don't it?" Mama asked.

I nodded. "Yes'm, and I've gone and gotten myself in a mess with Daddy over it. I don't think he's like to forgive me for what I said to him yesterday about Parnell giving us money were he and Caroline to get married."

Mama reached across the table and put her hand atop of mine. "Give your daddy some time, honey. I suspect he knows you just hadn't thought the matter through, is all. You know, your daddy ain't tickled by this proposal, either. He wants Caroline to go to school."

"Then why's he letting Parnell come up here all the time?" I asked, tugging hard at a thread coming loose from my sleeve.

"Well, I'll tell you, honey, partly it's because we've tried to raise you children so that when you came of age you could make your own decisions in a clearheaded fashion, whether we agreed with your decisions or not. But I suspect your daddy has other reasons for letting Parnell court Caroline."

"What other reasons?" I asked.

Mama smiled. "When your daddy started courting me, my mama and daddy weren't too happy about it. A lot of folks thought your Granddaddy Caleb was an odd sort, always coming up with wild notions. Caleb Coe was famous for standing up in church one Sunday and saying we should all be outside admiring God's handiwork instead of cooped up in a musty old building and singing tired old hymns." Mama laughed at the memory of it, then stood up and walked over to the window and looked out across the yard.

"Your daddy was tame compared to

Caleb, but he was still a free thinker. All them Coe boys were, and Mama and Daddy didn't want me to have a thing to do with any of them. It took John Coe two years to convince my daddy to let him come to the house to call on me. I reckon your daddy remembers that well enough to feel the least bit of sympathy for Parnell."

I leaned back in my chair. "What about you, Mama? What's your thinking on the matter?"

Mama turned to face me. "Honey, what I think ain't important. Caroline's got to make up her own mind about things. I've got my opinions on the situation, of course, but I tend to keep my thinking to myself."

"Unlike some people you know?"

"That's right, honey," Mama said, laughing. "And some people I know need to be real sweet to their daddy for the next couple days if they want to get back into his good graces."

It took a little while for Daddy to like me again, but I known everything was fine between us a few nights later when he took out his guitar and asked me to sing "I Gave My Love a Cherry" with him. That's always been a favorite of ours, and we been singing it together since I was right little. After we finished, I give Daddy a little hug and he give me a little hug back. I thought then that nobody'd ever be able to take Amos away from us, not if me and Daddy had anything to do with it.

chapter 6

"Miz Coe, I don't know when I've tasted potato salad this good. You must be the best cook in Indian Creek, bar none. Now don't go telling my mama I said that!" Parnell Caraway leaned back in his chair and dabbed at his mouth with his napkin. Then he gave a big old grin to let us know what a regular feller he was, just happy as he could be to be eating my mama's good cooking.

"That's nice of you to say, Parnell," Mama replied, busying herself with brushing some crumbs from her skirt. "But I'm sure it ain't true."

"Now, Miz Coe, you don't have to be modest with me," Parnell said. "A man knows good cooking when he tastes it! Ain't that right, John?"

"I reckon so," Daddy told him, lifting a forkful of butter beans to his mouth. "I believe it's an ability that comes natural to most males."

It was just like Parnell Caraway to call my daddy by his first name. Now, my daddy was always telling folks to do just that — "Mr. Coe was my daddy," he liked to say. "You just go on and call me John" — but I thought it disrespectful for a boy of seventeen to be so familiar with his elders.

Parnell looked across the table, where Caroline was pushing some beans around her plate with a spoon. "Now I bet Miss Caroline takes after her mama in the cooking department, ain't that right?"

Caroline raised an eyebrow but didn't actually look at Parnell, keeping her eyes on her plate. "I suppose I've been known to make a pie or two in my day, but they ain't been nothing special."

"Don't you believe her for a minute," Daddy said, winking at Parnell. "Caroline can do some cooking when she puts her mind to it."

"Can we talk about something other than cooking?" I asked. "It's about the least interesting topic I can think of."

Mama frowned at me, but I just shrugged. I was telling the truth, after all.

"Didn't mean to bore you, Dovey," Parnell said. His tone was jovial, but there was a note of something else in it, like he'd be just as happy if I'd keep my mouth shut. "What would you care to talk about? World events? Mathematics? Baseball?"

I give Parnell my most dire look. "If it's all the same to everybody, I'd prefer to be excused."

Mama nodded, so I carried my plate to the sink and signaled to Amos to follow me outside. To my surprise, Caroline came as well. "Good Lord," she said, sitting on the front stoop, spreading the flowered skirt of her dress out so it covered her legs. "That Parnell do go on."

"Whose idea was it for him to have supper here practically every night?" I asked, taking a seat beside Amos on the porch swing. "I know it weren't mine."

Caroline laughed. "I believe it was Parnell's idea. He's persistent, I'll give him that much."

Ever since Daddy had given his okay for Parnell to call on Caroline, Parnell had taken every advantage. It was like he lived with us. He showed up in the morning and helped Mama pull the chokeweed out of her garden, and then he'd go see what Daddy was up to in the barn. Midafternoon, he'd go back to his own house to change clothes, and forty-five minutes later you'd hear that automobile of his struggling up the mountain's twists and turns and know that Parnell had arrived for supper.

Parnell was endlessly polite to Mama and

friendly as could be with Daddy. He paid Caroline compliments whenever he got the chance to and did his best to tolerate me, though I did my best to try him.

As for Parnell's actions toward Amos, well, one thing was clear to me, and that was Parnell thought Amos was some sort of freak set loose from the circus. I could see it in the way that Parnell could hardly bring himself to look at Amos when they passed each other in the yard or were sitting across from one another at the table. It were as though Parnell thought deafness were contagious and you could catch it from just making eye contact. Parnell never made no effort to talk to Amos, even though it was perfectly clear that Amos could read lips. The rest of us chattered away to Amos, but Parnell couldn't even bring himself to say *boo*.

I wanted to point out this aspect of Parnell to Daddy, but I couldn't, of course. I certainly didn't want to make Daddy out of sorts with me again. Maybe I wouldn't have worried about it so much, except for that Daddy and Parnell seemed to be turning into fast friends. It seemed like any bad feeling Daddy might have had toward Parnell had gone and disappeared.

I heard Parnell asking Daddy's advice

over every little thing. "Now, John, tell me this, why is it when it's been raining outside my car will just plain cut off when I apply the brake to slow down?" Or, "John, explain me something. My mama's got a faucet that ain't done nothing but drip for two months now, but no manner of tightening up the pipes has any effect on it." Of course, my daddy being a fix-it man, he loved to tell folks how to repair all their broke-down things and could go on for quite a spell explaining this and that.

"Ain't it a pleasant evening," Parnell said, joining us on the porch, stretching out his arms like he'd like to take the night air into his embrace. "Your mama ought to be out here enjoying this, Dovey. Why don't you go on in and help her with them supper dishes?"

"Excuse me?" I could barely hold my fists to my sides. Only the fact that Parnell was close to a foot taller than me kept me planted to my seat. "You thinking that you're my daddy now? You think you're some kind of boss around here?"

Parnell laughed a long, smooth laugh. "No, I'm just making a suggestion, Dovey. You go on and do whatever you please. I just thought you might want to treat your mama sweet ever once in a while."

"I don't see you treating your mama too sweet," I replied. "Sitting up here and bad-mouthing her cooking the way you do."

"Oh, Dovey," Caroline said, joining Parnell in his laughter. Apparently, something about my behavior tickled her. "Now Parnell didn't say anything bad about his mama's cooking. He just was being polite, like a good guest."

I stood up. "Whose side you on, Caroline?"

"This ain't a war, Dovey," Caroline said in an even tone, which is how I known I was starting to irritate her. "I'm just pointing some things out to you."

My chin had dropped near to my chest, and my mouth was wide open. Here was Caroline Coe sticking up for Parnell! It was like she had been going fifty miles an hour in one direction and then turned around lickety-split and started going in the other!

Parnell had taken the opportunity to sit next to Caroline on the step. "Little sisters," he said, laughing. "They do get excited real easy about the littlest things, don't they?"

My face went hot. I could barely abide being compared to Parnell's sister, Paris. Me and Paris went back a long way, but we was never friendly with each other, despite the similarity of our ages. Paris ran around with two other girls from our school, Lorelei Parks and Rhondetta Simmons, and they spent most of their time commenting on the latest styles and who had the shiniest hair of all the girls in Indian Creek. I for one did not hold Paris in high regard.

Caroline did not seem to mind the topic of little sisters, however. "Lord, I can't tell you how many times Dovey . . ." I let the screen door slam behind me so as to not hear the rest of this conversation. I could tell it weren't going in any good direction.

Amos followed me back inside and into the kitchen, where Mama was still cleaning up the mess from supper. It about killed me to pick up a rag and help her, but us Coes ain't raised to sit around while another does all the work. Amos give me a scowl, like he thought I was following Parnell's orders.

"Now, you ought to know better than that, son," I told him, returning him scowl for scowl. Then I threw my rag at him and picked up another.

"Know better than what, Miss Dovey?" Mama asked as she walked past juggling three empty plates and the breadbasket.

"Parnell was out there telling me I ought to come in and help you, and now Amos is acting like I'm doing exactly like Parnell said."

Mama settled her load down on the countertop next to the sink. "That was nice of Parnell to think of such a thing, I reckon."

I dragged my rag down a long stretch of table. "If Parnell's so salt-of-the-earth nice, I suspect he'd be in here helping himself." I turned to repeat this comment to Amos, and I can report that it about bust him up laughing.

Me and Amos spent the best part of the next half hour helping Mama wash and dry and put away the dishes. I was the whole time praying that Parnell wouldn't walk in and take the notion that I was following his orders. But when I returned to the porch to see what them two was up to, I wished Parnell would've come in after all.

It weren't a pretty picture out there on that porch. Oh, the stars was shining, and the crickets was playing their little tune, and the breeze washed the good smell of honeysuckle across the evening. But the pleasure of all that was ruined by the sight of Parnell Caraway's arm around my sister's shoulder.

"Honey, we're going to have such a good time in Asheville, you would not believe it," Parnell was saying. "There's a restaurant I'm going to take you to that you're going to love. It's where all the real classy folks go."

I swear to you, my heart sunk in my chest right then and there. It had finally happened. Parnell had finally figured out a way into Caroline's heart. Here was a girl whose biggest dream was to leave home for the excitement of big-city restaurants and cultivated folks. I don't know how Parnell managed to stumble across this fact, but as soon as he did, he took advantage of it. And Caroline couldn't see that there were better ways out of town than in Parnell's car. My head began to pound. "Caroline, have you gone and lost your senses?" I cried. "You ain't going to Asheville with the likes of Parnell Caraway!"

Caroline just laughed at that. She looked over her shoulder at me and said, "Dovey, you are a child. You are twelve years old. But somehow you think you run this family, telling everybody what to do, leading Amos around by the hand, getting into everyone's business. Well, let me be the one to tell you, this ain't none of your business. So go on and get out of here."

Now us Coes don't let the hard words of others hurt our feelings, but I got to admit I felt like I'd been stung by a wasp when Caroline said them things. I looked at her a minute before I turned to go inside, but I tell you it was like gazing upon a stranger.

chapter 7

I began studying the matter of rich and poor, seeing as how most folks thought having money was the be-all to end-all and would make for a happy life. I weren't against having money by a long stretch. There'd been plenty of times when I'd like to have heard the jingle of silver in my pocket. But I weren't convinced being rich brings satisfaction to a person. And I didn't think it would bring satisfaction to Caroline, neither.

Most folks in Indian Creek was poor, and even the rich ones would probably only be medium if they moved somewheres like Charlotte or Winston-Salem. But I never heard of no one starving to death, and most parents managed to get a new pair of shoes for their children once a year or so.

Us Coes stood on the poorer side of the line, but we made do right well. We had us a fine house that my Granddaddy Caleb built years and years ago, and although the weather sometimes got inside, it was still a place to be proud of. The kitchen was big enough for all of us to gather comfortably without stepping on each other's toes, and there was nothing I liked better on a winter's day than to warm myself against the woodstove that stood in the corner. Mama was all the time warning me that I was going to burst into flames one day the way I leaned so close to the fire, but I didn't pay her no mind.

Our house had three bedrooms, and there were them about these parts who thought having three bedrooms was right extravagant. A lot of them at school had to share a room with three or four of their brothers and sisters, and a few slept in the same room as their mama and daddy. But Granddaddy Caleb was a man who liked his privacy, so he built a house where people could spread out some. Mama and Daddy's bedroom was off the kitchen, and the rooms that Amos, Caroline, and me had were off the parlor room. I shared a room with Caroline, which weren't so bad, except that Caroline was a neat one and got mad about the messes I made. Amos, being the only boy, got his own room, but he liked being at the center of things when he was in the house, so usually you'd find him in the kitchen.

The kitchen was always stocked with plenty of food. Every spring we planted a garden with peas, beans, tomatoes, corn, and potatoes, plus a few other things I'm probably forgetting, and Mama put me and Caroline to canning when the garden come to fruition. We had a root cellar, where we kept the potatoes, and a pantry off the kitchen with shelves to hold all our canned goods.

We kept chickens and two milk cows, Annie and Bess, so we had all the eggs and milk and butter we needed, and ice cream in the summer for special occasions, the Fourth of July and such. We also kept pigs, but that was a matter of some debate. I was the main debater, which would come as no surprise to them who known me well.

The problem started up when I become friendly with the pigs, giving them the names of Henrietta, Scarlett, King Edward, and Ralph. Anyone raising livestock to butcher will tell you that was a grave mistake on my part. Don't name anything you or someone else, say, your daddy, aims to kill. You can get right attached to an animal, especially if it's a pig.

Pigs are right smart, smarter than dogs, some will say. They come when you call them and will learn to do tricks easy. King Edward was especially gifted in this regard. I am also of the belief that pigs can understand most everything you say once you talk to them a while and they get a chance to learn your language.

I got the idea in my head that I would have me a pig circus and charge folks a dime to see it. I figured I'd keep half the money I made for myself and give the other half to Mama for her to buy material for a new dress, which she'd been badly in need of for some time. I even come up with a plan to ask Mama for her old sewing scraps so I could make some pig costumes with little sparklies all over them.

One night at dinner, I decided to tell Mama and Daddy of my idea, thinking they'd be real taken by it. Well, the first thing Daddy done once he stopped laughing was say, "When you aim to put this circus on? You best do it before first frost, 'cause them pigs will be gone to slaughter once it turns cold."

Now, I guess I known them pigs would be butchered sooner or later, but I reckon I kept that bit of knowledge way in the back of my head, where I wouldn't come across it. I started to thinking on the fact that King Edward, Scarlett, and all the rest would be on the breakfast table before too long, and the thought was like to tear me apart. I could see their little eyes, which weren't at all beady like some folks will tell you, and the way they ran on their little pig feet to greet me when I come to the barn of a morning.

"Daddy," I said to him, "I reckon we ought not to kill them pigs. I been working them so hard, their meat's bound to be all tough on the inside. I don't believe they's good eating pigs anymore."

Daddy leaned back in his chair, his eyes lit up by merriment. "What you reckon we ought to do with them pigs, then, Sister? I can't afford to feed any stock that ain't producing for us."

"I'm telling you, Daddy, that circus will make us a lot of money."

Daddy nodded his head, giving the matter some thought. "How many times you figure folks will spend a dime to see a pig jump through a hoop? I suspect a man sees that once, he'll be satisfied the rest of his days that he's seen it enough."

Daddy had a point there, but I weren't ready to give up easy. "We could train them to hunt fancy mushrooms. I hear folks up north will pay a lot of money for such things."

"Sister, you do take all." Daddy laughed. "No, I suspect them pigs will be bacon come fall."

That ended the matter for the time being, but I went on to argue for the pigs whenever I took a mind to. Of course, it was too late for Henrietta, Scarlett, King Edward, and Ralph. All I can say is that I ain't eaten bacon since, though I do find it difficult to pass up a piece of ham.

I never got too upset about Mama killing the chickens, I admit. It's hard to build up a head of steam for a chicken.

Our money come from here and there. Daddy most always had a fix-it-up job, so he brought in money pretty steady, though not a whole lot of it, on account that a lot of folks didn't have much money to pay him. Daddy didn't go to church, but Mama said he done his Christian duty by taking on jobs he known he wouldn't never get paid for doing.

Caroline helped out by doing some sewing and other little chores for Bridie Nidiffer, who was old and bent over and whose own children and grandchildren had moved off the mountain to find work in the city. Working for Bridie weren't the highest paying job in town, but it brought in a little extra change every week, and a little extra always helped.

Mama, Amos, and me did our part to bring in money by collecting roots and herbs to sell to doctors down in Wilkesboro and Hickory. There was all sorts of things growing in these parts: chamomile, foxglove, crampbark, dandelion, and, the best of all, goldenseal. Goldenseal would make you right wealthy, but it was hard to come by, and when you did find some, you had to be careful not to overpick, so there'd be some next time around. Mama said the problem was that most folks was greedy and they'd wipe off all the goldenseal from the side of a mountain if they come upon it.

Of the three of us, Amos was the best at finding roots and such. Once Mama taught him what to look for, he started spending his afternoons on the mountain searching things out. Amos was big and strong for his age, and it weren't nothing to him to climb and ramble through the hills for hours on end. Lots of times, he'd spend all day up there, which was why Daddy got Tom and Huck for him. They'd warn him if anything dangerous were about.

From what I could tell, Tom and Huck and Amos worked themselves out a kind of code. If Tom or Huck ever seen a thing they wanted Amos to take notice of, they put their nose in his hand and sort of nodded their heads toward whatever it was that got their interest.

Amos, on his part, made a collection of signals he used to talk to Tom and Huck with. I remember one afternoon, me and Amos was up on Katie's Knob looking for crampbark, which is good for soothing aches and whatnot. Amos clapped his hands three times, and Tom and Huck took off running.

"You trying to scare them dogs away?" I asked Amos. "That's too bad, because I don't reckon Daddy'll get you any more if you chase these ones off."

Amos grinned and rolled his eyes, to let me know what he thought of my jokes. A couple of moments later, Tom and Huck was back at our feet, and then just as quick they was off again. Amos nodded in the direction they'd run off to, and we followed them fifty yards through the woods, catching up with them at a bend in the creek where all sorts of weeds and flowers was growing. Though we didn't find any crampbark there, we did find a right nice patch of foxglove good for picking.

The way I seen things, us Coes had everything we needed in this world. Some might see us as poor, but that was their problem. We had saved up the money to send Caroline to college, which is more than many a richer family in town had done for their children. Parnell Caraway, for one, would not be packing his bags to go off to an institution of higher learning anytime soon. And if he had his way, nor would Caroline.

To my way of thinking, Parnell was a prime example of riches not necessarily making a man satisfied with his life. He had just about everything he could want, plus a little extra. He had silk shirts and ten pair of shoes, a genuine cowboy hat from San Antonio, Texas, and an automobile his daddy bought him secondhand. But for all them things he had crowding up his life, he still walked around looking for new, shiny things to add to his collections, and Caroline was one of the items on his list.

For a while there, in those first days of August, it felt to me like all them I known were under a spell — except for me and Amos, of course. And Caroline, well, she floated through her days as though she might take to the air at any minute. The main picture I have of her from that time is her long hair whipping out the window of Parnell's automobile as they drove down the road and off to Asheville. She was living the grand life of her dreams, and Mama and Daddy was letting her do it. Oh, I'd see Mama worrying her hands when Caroline drove off in that car, but she was staying true to herself and keeping out of Caroline's business. Myself, I thought this foolishness ought to be stopped, but I'd said my piece once, back in July, and no one seemed to heed it.

Parnell took Caroline's change of feeling toward him as a victory. I could hardly stand to look at him, but he took every chance he could to get me by myself and give me a hard time, now that he thought he had won this particular war. One afternoon, when Caroline was helping Mama put supper on the table, Parnell turned to where I was sitting across the porch from him. I was deep involved in *Robinson Crusoe*, which is a right good story by Mr. Daniel Defoe.

"Why you read all them books for, Dovey?" he asked me, running a hand through his silky dark hair and trying to catch his reflection in the front window. "Why ain't you inside learning how to make supper so you can get yourself a man someday?"

"Maybe I don't want to get myself a man someday," I told him, not bothering to look up from my book.

"Well, I reckon that might be a good thing, come to think of it. I imagine a feller would have a hard time warming up to you.

71

It's a shame you didn't get none of Caroline's good looks."

"What's it to you, Parnell?" I asked, giving him the evil eye.

"It ain't a thing to me. I just been wondering if there's a reason you don't ever take a comb to your hair or put on a dress from time to time."

"Maybe it's 'cause I'm afraid if I start making myself look all pretty, you might lose your fool head and fall to worship at my feet," I said. "Fact is, you're going to need somebody new to be in love with once Caroline comes to her senses."

I seen I struck a nerve.

"You're crazy, Dovey, if you think for a minute I'd ever give you a second look. And Caroline ain't going to change her mind about me, I'll tell you that much. She knows a good thing when she sees it, I'd say."

I turned back to my book, saying, "Now that's a matter of opinion, ain't it, Parnell?"

Parnell stood to go into the house. "Don't you get smart with me, Dovey Coe," he said, his voice low and even. "I ain't got the patience for it." The door slammed loud behind him.

I put down my book and stretched out my legs, mulling things over. When it come to rich and poor, Parnell and his kind stood on the other side of the line from us Coes, that was for sure. And as far as I was concerned, he ought to have stayed right where he belonged.

chapter 8

It was at dinner on a Friday evening that Parnell got his own self in some serious trouble. He and Daddy had been making a joke about this and that, just acting the fools for the amusement of all seated at the table, when Parnell let loose his fatal words.

"Now tell me seriously, John," he said, wiping a tear of mirth from his eye, "did you really think Caroline was going to go on to teachers college? Or was you just playing along?"

Daddy give Parnell a curious look. "Why, Parnell, you make it sound like she's done gone and changed her plans. To the best of my knowledge, them folks still got my money over there, so I reckon *somebody's* going to college."

Parnell slapped his knee and hooted a bit. "Good God, John, ain't you been paying attention? Caroline ain't going anywhere."

"What're you saying, Parnell?" Caroline asked from across the table, a bit of love still left in her voice. "We never said anything about me not going to college. We never talked that way."

"Now, Caroline, honey, be reasonable," Parnell said, trying to get serious about the matter. "It don't make sense for you to go now. You ain't going to be a teacher. You're going to be Mrs. Parnell Caraway and sit in the lap of luxury all day."

Maybe if Parnell had left it at that, maybe if he and Daddy hadn't been cracking jokes and being silly all evening, the situation would have worked itself out. But Parnell couldn't leave things alone, and on that particular evening he was of a mind to laugh at everything.

"Besides, Caroline," he said, and here's where he started to giggling again, "were you really serious about being a teacher? I mean, I ain't ever seen you pick up a book of your own volition. I ain't even sure you can read." Now that right there really broke old Parnell up.

You just keep talking, Parnell, I thought to myself as I slathered about an inch of butter on a biscuit. For the first time in weeks, I seen me a little glimmer of hope. Parnell had just made himself a grave error, talking to Caroline that way. Like I've said, she was sensitive about folks thinking she weren't anything more than a pretty face.

Caroline had some pride, and Parnell had just wounded it. He might think he could sweet-talk his way out of it, but I had my doubts.

That's why it come as no surprise to me that Caroline agreed right away the next day when Daddy suggested we have a going-away party for our future teacher. Oh, I tell you, me and Amos was practically dancing all over the house at the news. It told us all we needed to know. Caroline had left the idea of Parnell Caraway in the dust and was going back to her old dreams. If Caroline was going to get out of town, it would be by her own devices, not in Parnell Caraway's car on an afternoon trip.

Later that afternoon, I got even more proof of this when Caroline was setting the table for supper and casually remarked, "Folks think I'm good-hearted, and I reckon I am, but that don't mean a man can't set my blood to boiling by saying the wrong thing."

"You talking about Mr. Parnell Caraway?" I asked, handing her the silverware, a grin breaking across my face.

"Oh, I believe you know exactly who I mean," Caroline replied, grinning her own grin.

Caroline still acted as sweet as could be to

Parnell. He kept coming to the house every day, and they both pretended like that dinner conversation had never taken place.

"Oh, I do think you're going to enjoy the party," she told Parnell one afternoon while he was sitting on the porch steps watching me and Caroline pluck dead petunia blooms from Mama's garden. "It's always such a treat to have a party at the end of the summer, don't you think? I'm hoping Mama'll make some strawberry ice cream. I think this will be the best end-of-the-summer party anyone's ever given!"

I noticed that Caroline didn't once refer to the party as her going-away party. There weren't no doubt in my mind she was up to something, I just couldn't figure out what.

"That sounds fine," Parnell agreed, using a toothpick to get some dirt from under his nails. "You better not eat too much ice cream, though. I don't want you losing that pretty figure of yours."

"Now don't you worry yourself over that, Parnell," come Caroline's cheerful reply. "I aim to keep my looks for as long as I can."

"Why you always got to say such things, Parnell?" I asked, tossing a bunch of the wilted blossoms toward his feet. "Caroline ain't your prize sow you're going to take to the fair so you can win a ribbon, you know."

Caroline patted me on the shoulder. "Oh, don't take Parnell the wrong way, Dovey. Besides, if I was Parnell's prize sow, I reckon he'd want me to eat till I was too big to fit in the front door!"

I shook my head. I'd known Caroline long enough to know that this cheerfulness of hers weren't for real. But I had no idea what she was up to.

Once I got wrapped up in making the plans for the party, I stopped giving the situation between Caroline and Parnell so much thought. We set the date for a few days before Mama and Daddy was to drive Caroline down to school. Luther McDowell and Gaither Sparks would play music so folks who was of mind to could dance and carry on, and Mama and MeMaw would fry up a batch of chickens to be served with slaw, biscuits, greens, and whatever anyone else cared to bring to supper.

A week before the party, Mama and Caroline sat down at the kitchen table and made out a list of who all to invite.

Caroline chewed on the end of her pencil, thinking out loud. " 'Course, we'll invite all the McDowells and the Sparkses, since Luther and Gaither will be playing. And Patty Brown and all her folks, so Dovey can dance with Wilson."

"I ain't dancing with no one, lessen Daddy asks me to," I said, trying to get her away from the idea that me and Wilson Brown was going to dance the night away together.

Mama smiled. "You dance with whoever you want, Dovey, though I expect you to use your good manners when you say no to an unwanted suitor," she said in her best 'I am teaching you how to be a lady' voice. "Caroline, write down the Byerses and the Mitchells, honey. They been real good to you. Oh, and don't forget Pastor Bean and Coreen Lovett."

Caroline wrote down the list of names in her careful script. "I can't think of who else to ask," she said when she was done.

"What about Parnell and his folks?" Mama asked, sounding surprised that Caroline hadn't brought them up.

"My goodness, I can't believe I forgot old Parnell," Caroline said, looking sly. She added the name "Caraway" to the list.

"We ain't inviting Paris!" I exclaimed. I weren't about to put up with Paris Caraway for an evening, and I'd just as soon skip Homer, Lucy, and Parnell, too. "Why, that'll ruin everything, Mama," I complained. "Them Caraways come up here and everyone's going to spend the entire time looking at their feet and then go home early."

"They ain't going to do no such thing, Dovey," Mama replied. "Besides, I don't rightly see how we can overlook them, seeing as Parnell's practically lived here all summer. It wouldn't be right not to invite them."

"Can we at least not invite Paris?" I asked.

Mama laughed, thinking I was fooling, but I weren't doing no such thing.

Me and Amos spent a good amount of time that next week getting things ready. To the best of my remembrance, us Coes had not had a party before, if you didn't count grandparents and aunts and uncles and cousins coming over after church on Easter Sunday for dinner, or to drink cider and eat popcorn and cookies on Christmas Eve. Mostly what me and Amos known about parties come from the books we'd read.

Daddy said the most helpful thing we could do was get the barn cleaned out before he started building a platform for Luther and Gaither to play music on. I liked spending time in the barn, for the good smell of it, in part — the hay kept stored up in the loft and the sharp scent of the kerosene Daddy used to keep his tools clean. Them smells took me back to the days when nobody cared if I was acting like a lady or not, when I spent hours every day watching Daddy fix things up and being his little helper.

By the day before Caroline's party, me and Amos had gotten the barn swept and Daddy's tools and such put over to the side of the barn in an orderly fashion and covered up with some old blankets so they wouldn't be an eyesore. There weren't much left to do but to commence decorating the place. Here's where being more girlish than I naturally was would have come in handy, I reckon. If I'd been studying up on ladylike activities, I might have been able to sew some curtains to hang over the windows or some such thing.

It was Amos who come up with the idea of making paper chains to hang all over the place in a festivelike manner. We got us a mess of colored paper and old comic books we'd read so many times that we could probably draw our own copies, and we cut them into colorful strips to make chains with.

"This will be a sight to see," I told Amos as I added a loop to the chain I was working on. It already stretched halfway across the barn floor.

Amos nodded, then held up one finger, as if to tell me to wait a minute. Dragging his paper chain behind him, he run over to the little room that held Daddy's worktable and chair and closed the door. A few seconds later, he popped back out, that chain wrapped around him from head to foot. He looked like a Christmas tree all done up in decorations.

"Son, you are a crazy thing!" I said, admiring his handiwork.

"If Amos ain't careful, a lot of folks are going to think he's crazy."

Parnell stood at the doorway, his fingers hooked in his suspenders, smiling down on our little scene. "I reckon a lot of folks already do," he said. "I've heard many a story myself. I hear Amos used to like to go around and kill people's chickens. Why do you suppose he did that?"

I was glad of only one thing right then, and that was that Parnell was facing me and not Amos. I preferred that Amos not be privy to this particular conversation.

"You're the one who's crazy if you believe them kind of stories," I told Parnell, turning back to my work, pretending like his words hadn't affected me. "You ought not to spread rumors. They'll come back around to bite you in your behind."

Parnell laughed a dry laugh. "Don't blame me that some folks have their concerns about the boy. Besides, I ain't the one making up the stories."

"No, you're the one going around repeating them."

"I just think you ought to know that there's some folks out there who don't feel real comfortable with Amos around, is all," Parnell said, turning to leave. "I'd advise your brother to be real careful about acting the fool. He could get himself in trouble."

By this time, Amos had pulled the paper chain from around him. He looked at me and shrugged his shoulders, as if to ask what the problem was. I shrugged my shoulders back at him, like I couldn't figure out what Parnell was going on about.

Amos smiled, then picked up the end of his chain and started running around in circles so that it was flying like a tail behind him. Parnell shook his head, like only a crazy boy would do such a thing, then walked off toward the house.

I felt the blood run hot through me, and I wanted to hit something as hard as I could. But for Amos's sake, I shook off my bad feelings and give him a smile as he run in silly circles around the barn.

The worst thing about Parnell's little

warning is I known it was true. There had always been folks around Indian Creek who believed Amos was off-kilter. That's one reason I made a point from the time we was little to take Amos to town with me, so folks could see that he was as normal as any other boy except for the fact of his not being able to hear. And while there was always going to be some mean boy to make fun of Amos, I thought that most folks had taken to him and liked him.

Parnell's the only one who don't like Amos, I thought to myself as I pulled the length of my paper chain toward me. Parnell is the only one who'd rather have him out of the picture.

I would have to be extracareful to watch over Amos from now on, that much was for sure. Somebody had to protect him from the likes of Parnell Caraway.

chapter 9

The day of the party broke cool and pretty, and I woke up hardly able to wait until evening, when folks would start coming over. MeMaw and PawPaw, Mama's mama and daddy, come around noon, and MeMaw started baking her fancy chocolate cakes she only made for company. You got to be quick around one of MeMaw's cakes, else you won't get a bite. They get et up in a flash. I tried sticking my finger in the mixing bowl when I thought MeMaw weren't looking, but she caught me and swatted my hand away, saying, "Law, Dovey, you're getting to be too old for such doings."

"I'm only twelve, MeMaw," I told her. "I got me a few years before I turn into an old woman."

"But you're a young woman now, and you best start acting like one. I reckon a lot of boys will be after you 'fore too long. Caroline was just telling me that Wilson Brown's right sweet on you."

"Caroline's got a head full of dreams,

MeMaw," I said. "Don't go listening to her."

I decided I best leave the kitchen before I got surrounded by a flock of women wanting to talk about me and Wilson Brown. I walked out to the barn, where Daddy and Amos was building the little platform for Luther and Gaither to play on.

The only time I felt real bad about Amos not being able to hear was when I listened to music. It was right difficult to explain to Amos what music was, the same way it was hard to get across to him that when people moved their mouths to talk, sound came out. He didn't have a good idea for sound, I don't think. The closest I could get him to understanding was for him to put his hand on my throat while I talked. When you talk, your throat will vibrate a bit, and I wanted Amos to feel that particular vibration. The next day I heard him making them noises he made from time to time, and when I looked into his room, he had his hands on his throat, listening to himself.

I hoped Amos would be okay with all them folks around. I knew it could be confusing for him to have a lot of folks about him moving and talking all at once. Watching him help Daddy build that platform, I got to wondering if some little girl might take a shine to him soon. Amos was right handsome; in fact, he had a lot of the same features as Caroline had, and even went one better. His hair was yellow and curly while Caroline had to do with dark and straight. How I got stuck with this old brown mess on top of my head, I don't know. Seems God made me for something other than sitting around and looking good all the time, I reckon.

I sat down on a pile of old blankets for a minute, letting my usual worries wash over me. What if some little girl broke Amos's heart? What if Parnell turned Caroline's feelings around again and convinced her to marry him and then somehow got control of Amos and sent him to a home? What if something happened to me and there was no one to help Amos through all the complications that life threw in his path?

"Sister, come over here and help hammer some of these nails," Daddy yelled from where he and Amos was working. I stood up then and shook the worries from me. When I reached the other side of the barn, Daddy put a hammer in my hand, saying, "Just don't tell your mama I made you stray from your ladylike ways. I'll get in a mess of trouble for that."

I began pounding a nail into the two-by-four, humming beneath my breath, and in less than a minute, I felt like my old self again.

Hammering will always cure what ails you, I have found.

After what seemed like years, the sun started making its way down the other side of Katie's Knob, and us Coes got dressed for the party. Caroline looked pretty as always in a blue and white polka-dot dress and sweet little white dance slippers Mama ordered special from the Sears and Roebuck catalog. Mama looked extrapretty, too. She had on her red dress that brought out the coppery red lights in her hair, which is brown like mine, only darker.

I was hoping to get by with wearing a clean pair of dungarees and a white shirt, but Mama come into my room and said I had better wear a dress so as to make Caroline happy. She pulled out my good yellow dress from where I tried to keep it hid in the back of the closet, and then went to borrow a yellow ribbon for my hair from Caroline. By the time I finished getting ready I looked so dolled up, I hardly known myself in the mirror.

Seems like just about everybody showed up at once, and the yard was full of folks talking and laughing and looking good as they known how to. Tom and Huck was running around, trying to convince folks to give them the scraps off their plates, and a couple of the littler children were chasing after them. I sat on the porch with Amos and Wilson Brown, feeling like I was in another girl's skin. For the first time since I known him, I felt like I needed to make nice conversation with Wilson. That's what wearing a dress will do to a person.

By the time most folks were well into their eating, who should finally show up in his car but Parnell Caraway. I breathed a bit more easy when I seen he come alone. The last thing I wanted was for Paris to see me dressed like I was. She'd never let me hear the end of it.

Parnell strolled up to the yard, nodding and smiling at folks left and right, like he were a politician. A few of the younger girls got right fluttery, chirping out, "Well, hey there, Parnell," as he passed. I seen Parnell wink at a few of them, and they liked to never stop giggling.

Caroline give Parnell a wave, and a couple girls sitting next to her on the steps scooted over to make Parnell room. He sat down next to Caroline like a king taking his throne.

"You know what I heard Fetzer Hall tell

my daddy?" Wilson asked me, nodding over to where Parnell was making a fuss over my mama's fried chicken.

"What's that?" I asked, relieved to be getting a conversation going instead of just sitting there looking fancy.

Wilson leaned over close to me. "He said a bunch of them were up to Buddy Webb's a-drinking Friday night, and Parnell was there, too, just throwing whiskey down his throat like it were water. Well, in wanders old Cypress Terrell, just to get in from the weather, is what Fetzer told my daddy. Cypress weren't going to make trouble for no one."

I nodded my head.

"Well, Parnell starts saying things to Cypress," Wilson continued. "First just conversational type sayings, like, 'There's a whole lotta thunder out there tonight, ain't there, Cypress,' like that. But then he starts getting real mean, saying folks like Cypress and his mama ought to just wander off into the woods and get lost and stop being such a burden on society. Fetzer said Parnell went so far as to take off his belt like he was going to beat Cypress with it, but Buddy got aholt of him, and some of the other fellers got Cypress out of there."

I looked at Parnell over there on the steps,

talking gay as could be with Caroline and them other girls, and felt a chill of fear in me. How a man could seem so nice and neighborly on the outside and be up to no good on the inside, well, it made me wonder about everybody in the world.

Folks started making their way over to the barn once they heard Gaither and Luther tuning up their fiddles. Gaither and Luther started up with "Little Red Rooster," then played a few more numbers before folks convinced Daddy to do the calling for a dance. That got about everybody out on the floor except for a few of the older folks. Even me and Wilson got in the swing of it, do-si-doing and bowing to our partners.

I guess the playing went on for right about an hour when Gaither and Luther said they was going to take themselves a break. Most folks leaned against the wall to catch their breath and sent their little ones to fetch them a glass of lemonade. A few of the men stepped outside the barn to smoke. Wilson asked me if I felt like taking a walk to cool down, and I saw that as being a fine idea, so we headed over toward the pond down to the north end of the house.

What happened next surprised me so, I barely known what to make of it. Wilson reached over and grabbed my hand real casual, like it were the most natural thing in the world for him to do. I looked around to make sure no one was watching, and when I figured no one seen us, I let myself relax into the feel of his hand holding mine. I ain't ashamed to say I right enjoyed it.

We stood at the edge of the pond for some time not saying anything, just letting our hands swing back and forth. The crickets chirped, and the frogs talked back and forth to each other. I could see a trace of a silver moon in the darkening sky, and I smelled the sweet scent of the honeysuckle growing in a tangle over to the house. Finally, Wilson cleared his throat a bit and said, "You look real pretty tonight, Dovey."

I give his hand a little squeeze and said, "So do you. I mean, handsome. You look right handsome, Wilson Brown."

I could feel my face going red from me telling Wilson Brown he looked pretty. But he didn't seem to mind none. In fact, he leaned over and kissed me real light on the lips. I couldn't believe how soft his mouth was, like a butterfly passing over my face.

I couldn't think of anything to say after that, so I leaned over and kissed Wilson back. We held that kiss a bit longer, then broke apart and looked straight at each other. I noticed for the first time how nice his eyes were, dark brown with little flecks of green inside.

"I reckon we ought to head on back before they start to miss us," Wilson said. He give me another quick kiss, and we walked up to the barn, not holding hands this time, because there were others about, but sort of rubbing shoulders nonetheless.

When we got to the barn, Gaither and Luther was tuning up again, and Daddy had his guitar out. Folks was milling about, ready to move their feet again and looking forward to hearing Daddy pick a little. Just as Daddy started to head to the stage, Parnell jumped right in front of him and stood dead center on the platform.

"Could I have everybody's attention, please?" he yelled out real loud. "Folks! If I could have your attention for a minute, I'd sure appreciate it!"

Everybody quieted down right quick. Parnell looked over the crowd like he was king of us all. "Caroline Coe, would you please come up here?"

Caroline made her way to where Parnell stood, her head held up in the air. I could see by her shaky smile, though, that Parnell was making her nervous.

Parnell give her a big grin, like to say, "Don't you worry about nothing," and turned back to give us his announcement. "Now, when I come here tonight, I didn't have no idea this was a going-away party for Caroline. To be honest, I had it fixed in my mind that Caroline ain't going away. I know none of you all want to see Caroline go on to teachers college, now do you? Especially since everybody knows that a little learning is wasted on someone as pretty as Caroline."

Voices buzzed throughout the barn, then quieted down. Everyone waited to hear what Parnell would say next.

"I think all of us would like to see Caroline spend the rest of her days here in Indian Creek, and I aim to make that happen," Parnell said, taking hold of Caroline's hand. "That is why I am taking this opportunity, here in front of our entire community, to make a most formal proposal to Miss Caroline Coe. Caroline, I am asking you to be my wife, here tonight, for the last time. What do you say, honey? Won't you marry me?"

Parnell pulled a ring from his pocket and held it to the light coming from a high window. It was clear to everyone there that it was a diamond Parnell was offering Caroline. A murmur ran through the room. Lots of folks looked over to Daddy to see if he known this was going to happen, but he just stood there with his arms crossed over his chest, his face not betraying a bit of whatever he might be thinking.

I could tell by Caroline's expression that she was as confused as everyone else, that she hadn't been expecting this proposal for one minute. That's when it finally come clear to me what she'd been up to. She'd probably figured this being a going-away party and all, Parnell would get the point and head on home. But old Parnell was craftier than that. It didn't surprise me in the least bit that he'd decided to have the last word on the matter.

"Come on, Caroline," he prodded after Caroline had kept her silence for several moments. "Say you'll stay here and be my pretty thing. Don't go waste yourself on being a teacher."

That's when Caroline's confusion bloomed into fury. She started shaking her head back and forth, almost like there were a song she was keeping time to. "No, Parnell," the words finally come out of her, her teeth clenched tight. "No, I don't believe I'd marry you if you were the last man on earth."

chapter 10

Well, you might could imagine the expression on Parnell's face when he heard Caroline turn him down in a way that left no doubt as to where she stood on the matter. He looked like someone had reached down through his throat and pulled his guts right up out of it.

Someone yelled from the crowd, "Don't be shy now, Caroline, tell the man how you feel!" Everybody laughed good and hard at that. Almost everybody, that is. Neither Parnell nor Caroline let on that they heard.

Parnell looked Caroline up and down like he were sizing her up for the first and last time. "Fine, then, if that's the way you feel about it," he told her, his voice rising to a high pitch. "To hell with you, Caroline Coe!"

Daddy moved up on him real quick then, but Parnell was already headed for the door. When he got there, he turned and looked at us. "To hell with all of you," he yelled. Then he shoved his way past Amos and was out the door, and a minute later come the sound of his car starting up and heading down the road into the night.

"That boy don't take too well to rejection, do he?" someone asked in a real amused tone. Then all sorts of voices started talking, working out amongst themselves what had just happened.

Caroline walked out of that barn just as normal and steady as you please, but her face was still red with fury. Soon as she walked out the door, Mama and MeMaw hurried out after her.

Daddy climbed up the platform and spoke quietly to Luther and Gaither, who commenced to playing again. But it was easy to see that the spirit had gone out of things. About an hour or so later, about the time the summer twilight faded, folks started gathering up their families and trickling out of the barn a little at a time. Wilson Brown come over to me to say good-bye. "You want to meet me at the farmers market on Saturday?" he asked. "We could maybe pass an afternoon looking at the sights."

"Sure," I told him. "I'd like that right much."

It took us Coes a long time to settle into sleep that night. Caroline went right up to bed after talking some with Mama and MeMaw, but the rest of us sat out on the porch, not quite sure what to do with ourselves. Daddy picked at his guitar a little, but you could tell his thoughts was somewhere else.

"I reckon Parnell thought he was going to force that little girl's hand, proposing to her in front of all them folks that way. I suspect he didn't count on Caroline being as stubborn as a mule, now did he?" he spoke at last, looking out into the yard where fireflies was lighting up the night one spot at a time.

Mama leaned forward in her chair, a pained look on her face. "Caroline made her point this evening, I'll give her that much. But why she couldn't have told Parnell she weren't going to marry him before all this is beyond me."

"Well, like the man said, this too shall pass." Daddy leaned his guitar up against the house so he could stand and stretch. "We'll get Caroline down to school on Saturday, and pretty soon we can all forget it ever happened."

"I just wish there were some way to stop folks from talking about it," Mama said, knotting her fingers together with the worry of it all.

Daddy laughed. "Shoot, woman, this is

the best thing that's happened to most of them folks all year! Besides, what do we care what they say? Caroline didn't ask that boy to go and make a fool of hisself that way. This weren't our fault. Any man who says a bad word about us, he ought to remember whose chickens he was eating."

Mama give Daddy a long look then, like she was none too happy with him. Sometimes Daddy forgot that just because he didn't care none what folks thought about him didn't mean that Mama felt the same way. Mama had some high standards Daddy didn't always share, and sometimes their differences in that regard got them to feuding.

"All I got to say is that Parnell Caraway has done nothing but try to tear this family apart all summer," I said, standing to go inside to bed. "As far as I'm concerned, he done got what he deserved." I'd been dying to say that very thing since the conversation started, and it felt good to finally get the words out of my throat.

Daddy laughed. "I don't know that you're right about Parnell trying to tear the family apart, but it's hard to argue that the boy had it coming to him. That'll teach him to make one of them Coe women mad!"

"Honestly, John!" Mama said, rising from

her seat. "You'd make a joke out of the Second Coming." She followed me into the house, allowing the screen door to slam behind her.

"What did I tell you, son?" I heard Daddy say to Amos from the porch. "It don't pay to get any of them women mad."

The next few days ran pretty hectic, everyone trying to help Caroline get ready to go off to teachers college. There weren't a peep said about Parnell's proposal by anyone. Us Coes just pretended like that little incident fell right off the map. Besides, we had enough emotions in us about Caroline leaving that the rest of it washed out of our heads after a day or so, though later we'd think about it long and hard.

Me and Caroline had been sleeping in the same bed since Mama took me out of the crib, and it was beginning to hit me that pretty soon I'd be by myself in an ocean of blankets when Caroline was gone. For as long as I could remember, I'd been wishing for my own room where I could spread out my collections of things and enjoy looking at them instead of having to keep it all in a box so as not to get in Caroline's way. I had a good many arrowheads and thirty-two pieces of sugar quartz. Caroline was all the time complaining about the messes I made.

So you'd think I'd be happy about Caroline going off to school, but once it sunk in that she was really going, I begun to feel right badly about it. I'd spent all my life going to sleep with the scent of her floating over me, roses and soap and something without a name that was just Caroline's particular smell. It made me feel all cozy and safe when I was real little to put my face in her pillow and breathe in deep.

I think everybody felt the same way I did. I caught Mama once or twice getting weepy over a sink full of pots and pans, and when I asked Daddy to pick a little on his guitar, he said he just weren't in the right spirits for music making. Even Tom's and Huck's ears were drooping a little low, it seemed to me. Amos stayed to the house every day after the party until Daddy put Caroline's things in the back of the truck and said it was time to go. That was right odd behavior for Amos, who would head out to Katie's Knob even when there was two foot of snow outside.

The night before Caroline left for school, she and I had us a real heart-to-heart talk, something we didn't do too often like some sisters will, on account of how we're real different in ways. But I wanted for us to be square on the matter of Parnell Caraway.

"Did you ever once consider marrying Parnell?" I'd asked her after Mama'd turned off the lights and pulled the door closed behind her.

Caroline was quiet a long while. "Well, to answer your question, yes, I did from time to time consider marrying Parnell. I sure did like riding over to Asheville with him and going to restaurants. That was something. I thought maybe after I finished college that me and Parnell could have us a nice house somewhere and live a fine life. You know, he was real sweet to me most of the time."

She paused, like she were remembering the good times she had shared with Parnell. But when she spoke again, it was clear those times held no truck with her in the light of more recent events. "But, law, when he made that remark about me being too dumb to be a teacher, well, that was it. How could a person say such a thing? You don't believe that, do you?"

I scrambled to come up with a reply. "Remember how you helped Lonnie Matthews with his math problems at school?" I asked. "Only a real smart person could have helped someone as stupid as Lonnie. It shows you'd make a right good teacher."

Caroline reached over and petted me on the shoulder. "I appreciate you for saying that, Dovey. I ain't — I'm not — claiming to be some brilliant scientist or some such thing. But I swear I get tired of folks only paying attention to how I look."

I decided it was best not to point out that Caroline made use of her looks whenever there was something she coveted and could use her good looks to get. I was fairly certain such a remark would not be appreciated.

"I just wish Parnell wouldn't have made me so mad when he proposed," Caroline said after a moment, her voice full of regret. "I hadn't meant to be so harsh when I told him no. It just came as such a big surprise, that proposal of his coming when it did, in front of the entire county. I thought he'd seen what a joke I'd played on him with that party, and that would be that. I didn't reckon on him pulling a ring out of his pocket."

With that, she turned to the wall and went to sleep. Me, I stayed awake for quite some time after, rethinking the events of the evening, relishing the scene of Caroline's rejection of Parnell, even if Caroline did regret it. If he'd been dreaming of being the boss of me and sending Amos away, his dreams was dead and gone now. I admit for a slip of a second, I almost felt sorry for Parnell getting humiliated that way, but I got over it right quick.

The plan was for Mama and Daddy to take Caroline down to Watauga County, which was about an hour away from us, on Saturday and stay over at Daddy's cousin Ray's house in Deep Gap that night. Me and Amos would go down to MeMaw and PawPaw's in town at nightfall and go to church with them on Sunday. Mama and Daddy aimed on being back in time for Sunday dinner.

I always enjoyed staying at MeMaw and PawPaw's house. MeMaw was a right good cook, and she always gave us biscuits and sausage gravy for breakfast, which is my favorite. She kept her kitchen full of all kinds of cookies for her grandbabies. At least that's who she claimed them cookies was for. MeMaw was right famous for her sweet tooth. She liked to keep a handful of gingersnaps or Mexican wedding cakes, which are them little powdered cookies that sort of fall to pieces in your mouth, wrapped in a napkin in her purse. She'd feed you one if you started getting restless in church, and she'd eat one herself just to keep you company.

Saturday morning we all got up good and early to send Caroline off. Mama packed her and Daddy and Caroline a breakfast of biscuits and preserves to eat while they was driving, and told me and Amos to fix ourselves a breakfast of whatever we pleased, just make sure to do the dishes after.

Me and Amos helped Daddy bring down Caroline's trunks to the truck and then stood on the porch to say our good-byes. Caroline looked real nice in her traveling suit and a matching hat, but I could tell she had butterflies knocking around in her stomach. I felt right funny myself, like a rock had caught in my throat. My eyes got real watery when I give Caroline a hug good-bye, but it might have just been that perfume she was wearing that made a few tears slip out from me.

I thought of our talk as I watched Caroline ride away down the mountain. I was sad to say farewell, but maybe it was best that she was going away for a while. She needed to get rid of the ill feelings Parnell had filled her with. In the meantime, the rest of us Coes could get back to normal, now that Parnell was gone from our lives.

That was one good thing about this whole mess, I thought, waving at the truck. At least Parnell Caraway wouldn't want to have no more to do with my family. He'd be leaving us alone from now on, that much was for sure.

As it turned out, I had underestimated Parnell Caraway's intentions considerably.

chapter 11

Tom and Huck ran after Daddy's truck as it made its way down our road, something between a bark and a moan coming out of their mouths. I turned to Amos to ask him what he wanted to eat, even though I weren't feeling real hungry right then. I just wanted to get on and do something. Amos led me into the kitchen, where he pulled out the fixings for flapjacks. I made up a mess of them, and by the time they were cooking on the griddle, I had an appetite working in me. We piled our plates high and poured on the blueberry syrup, then went out to the porch to eat. Mama always made us eat at the table, so eating on the porch was kind of a vacation for me and Amos.

After we roamed through the house a bit, getting a feel for it emptied of everyone but ourselves, we decided to head on down to the farmers market to meet Wilson. I run a comb through my hair and made sure my shirt didn't have any spots, which was about as much of a beauty routine as I had. Amos was outside collecting Tom and Huck to drop them over to MeMaw's while we went to the market, and once I come down ready to go, the four of us went into town.

As soon as folks saw us on King Street, the ones who hadn't been to the party come over and asked a million questions. I felt a little like a movie star with all the attention I was getting, and hateful as it is to say, I weren't too upset that just about everybody known Parnell got the sass knocked out of him by a Coe.

"Is it true he got down on bended knee to propose in front of all them people?" someone asked me. Five or six folks were standing about us.

"Naw," I replied. "He would've gotten his pants dirty."

Everybody laughed. "Hey, Dovey." It was Curtis Shrew calling out to me. "You gonna take up with Parnell now that Caroline's gone off and left him?"

"You got to be kidding, Curtis," I told him. "I'd just as soon shoot him as look at him."

Paris Caraway made her way through the crowd of folks around me and Amos. She was dressed in a pair of tan English riding pants and tall, polished boots with flat heels.

"I see we got a new place for dumping trash," she said, a little smirk riding around her mouth.

"Then you best lay yourself down, Paris," I said. "The man'll be coming by soon to collect you."

Folks laughed at that, but they moved on just the same. Then it was just me, Amos, and Paris.

"You look like you're off to the foxhunt," I told Paris.

"And you look like one of them trashy Coes, which I guess you are," she replied. "I guess you're feeling mighty smart about the way your sister done Parnell."

"I don't feel one way or the other. And Caroline didn't do nothing to Parnell but tell him the truth. Truth hurts, I hear."

Paris was fixing her mouth to come back with a smart remark, but just then her mama called out from the doorway of Caraway's Dry Goods, "Paris! You get away from those children! I don't want to see you near the likes of them!"

I watched Paris's back as she strolled over to her daddy's store looking all high and mighty about herself. Amos patted me on the back, trying to calm me down. He started making some of his noises, and I looked over at him. He was moving his mouth at me. "Oh, oh," he said.

"It's okay," I said to him. "She's just a bunch of hot air dressed like a human being."

Amos nodded, then made a coughing noise. "Oh, oh," were the sounds he was making. He patted my back again. "Oh ca."

It hit me like a hand upside the head.

"Okay! Okay! Amos, you're saying 'okay'! You're talking!"

Amos smiled and sort of shrugged his shoulders, like there weren't nothing to it. I couldn't help dancing him around and hugging on him.

Wilson Brown came strolling up, a big grin on his face, carrying a bag of licorice sticks. "Y'all having another party? Or are you dancing from the sheer joy of seeing me?"

I commenced to telling him about Amos saying his first word, and Amos give him a demonstration. Wilson just shook his head and handed Amos the entire bag of licorice. "Ain't this a fine day," he said, and threw me another one of them grins.

Wilson was right, it was a fine day, even with the sadness of Caroline going off to school. Summer cools off a sight faster in the mountains than it does in other parts, and a light wind was lifting up our hair and blowing real soft on the back of our necks. It seemed like we spent most of the day just wandering, finding interesting things to look at at every turn. Big, puffy clouds filled up the sky, changing shape every so often, and we leaned our backs against the steps of the courthouse where we sat, telling each other stories about the pictures we saw.

I guess the only bad part of things was when we passed by Parnell leaning against his car, taking sips from a bottle in a bag and making time with a pretty girl by the name of Rebecca Kyle, who was two grades ahead of me in school. Her cheeks were all flushed, like Parnell had been sweet-talking her some.

"I guess he done got over Caroline right quick," I muttered to Wilson as we come toward the two of them.

"Hey, Dovey," Parnell called out like we was old friends. "Why ain't you wearing that yellow dress? You almost looked like a girl in that thing. It was the first time I ever looked at you twice."

Rebecca Kyle give out a little giggle at that.

"Don't get your hopes up, Parnell," I told him. "I ain't interested in the likes of you. That seems to be a trait among us Coe women, now don't it?"

Parnell's face got real red.

"Why don't you get yourself on home now, Dovey. Before that mouth of yours goes and gets you hurt real bad."

Wilson stood up for me then. "I expect you best not be threatening Dovey, Parnell. You might stand to get yourself in a mess of trouble."

Parnell laughed. "From who? You?"

Wilson squared off like he was ready for a fight, but I stepped in between him and Parnell.

"You already been licked once this week, Parnell," I said. "Ain't your face already red enough?"

Rebecca Kyle pulled on Parnell's arm. "Come on, let's go for that ride you were promising me. I ain't interested in watching no fight."

Giving a look that about sent a knife through me, Parnell shook off Rebecca and walked around to the other side of the car to open the door for her. Then he come back around and opened his own door, but before he got in, he turned back to me. "Don't you worry, Dovey Coe. You and me are going to have us a long talk real soon."

"I wouldn't mess with him too much, Dovey," Wilson said to me as we watched Parnell drive off. "I suspect he could make you right miserable."

"He's been making me miserable my entire life," I replied, trying to make a joke of it. "I don't know why he'd stop now."

The joy sort of trickled out of our afternoon after that. Wilson had to get on home for supper, and it was about time for me and Amos to head over to MeMaw's. Wilson said he'd see me the next day in Sunday school, and we said our good-byes.

Me and Amos started walking toward MeMaw's house, which was on the other side of town, toward Katie's Knob and home. Tom and Huck run up to us when we got up to MeMaw's front walk. MeMaw come out on the porch and called, "Hey, you'uns come in now! Supper's not but a half hour away! Amos, leave them dogs on the porch. I don't want them dirtying up my floors."

That's when I remembered I never brought our church clothes from home, and MeMaw would never let us into a house of God dressed the way we were.

"I got to go back to the house, MeMaw, and get our church clothes!" I called to her. "I'll be back directly." I run off real quick so she couldn't get ahold of me. MeMaw don't take kindly to folks being late for supper.

It was strange to come up to the house

and not see anyone moving about. It made me feel kind of lonely. When I went into the kitchen, it still smelled like flapjacks and syrup. I went into Amos's room and spent a good ten minutes searching for his Sunday shoes before I found them wadded up in an old sweater under his bed.

I was wondering if I ought to bring that yellow dress back with me for church the next day when I heard the sound of a car coming up the road. I figured MeMaw must've sent PawPaw to fetch me, so I walked out to the porch to give him a wave.

Parnell's car was pulling into the yard. Shoot, I thought, he's come to give me some trouble, and I'm up here all by myself. I checked my pocket for my knife. I was figuring I might need to use it.

chapter 12

But it weren't Parnell that stepped out of that car. It was Paris.

I blinked my eyes real fast a couple times to make sure I weren't seeing things, but sure as day, Paris Caraway was walking up our yard, still wearing them riding clothes she had on earlier. I reckoned that was the first time she'd ever stepped foot on our property. She come right up to the steps, but didn't go no farther once she saw me.

"I came to fetch you, Dovey," she said to me. "Parnell's got one of those dogs of yours locked up in the back room of the store, and he says you best come claim it before he takes a mind to do something about it."

"What's Parnell doing with one of Amos's dogs?" I asked.

"It wandered into the store, and when Parnell tried to shoo it on out, why, it tried to bite his hand off. You shouldn't be letting those mangy dogs run loose. They're dangerous."

I rubbed my head, trying to figure out

what was going on here. "So why'd he send you to fetch me?" I asked her.

"He's making sure that dog don't get out and hurt some child," Paris answered. She looked about her for the first time. "You need to paint this house. It's a sight."

"Maybe Daddy will hire you for the job," I said. "Maybe then you could afford to buy you some real pants."

"Just get in the car, Dovey. I ain't got all day."

I got into the front seat next to Paris, hating to admire the leather upholstery as much as I did. The inside smelled real good, like Parnell paid someone to sit in the car and smoke a pipe all day long. It didn't occur to me till we were halfway down the road that Paris was a bit young for driving, but I reckoned them Caraways didn't have to worry so much about following the rules as the rest of us.

Paris hummed a little tune as she drove, probably enjoying the thought of folks seeing her behind the wheel of her brother's car. I had to admit she looked right smart, driving with one hand while the other was resting on the back of the seat, like she'd been doing this all her life.

"I plan on getting out of Indian Creek one day," she said out of the blue, but it was like she were talking to herself as much as to me. "I reckon this town's too small for me," she went on. "I need a big city full of classy folks who know there's more to life than farming and quilting bees."

"Where you aim to go?" I asked, surprised to be in a normal conversation with her.

"Asheville, maybe," she replied. "Or maybe even further away. London, England, could be. I wouldn't mind getting as far from here as I can go."

It struck me as odd that Caroline and Paris might have some of the same dreams. Shoot, visiting London, England, even sounded like a good idea to me. Not that I was dying to move away from my family; just sometimes I wondered about what it would be like to see some of them foreign spots I'd been reading about in books. China always struck me as being real exotic, and Africa, too. I'd been considering saving up to go on one of them safaris one day, maybe ride me an elephant.

"I wouldn't mind going to London, England, myself," I told her. "See where they keep them kings and queens."

Paris looked over to me and give out a little laugh. "How do you plan to get there? Ride over on one of them pigs of yours?"

The conversation kind of sputtered out

between us after that. I guess Paris figured she'd told me as much about herself as she wanted me to know. We drove by MeMaw's house, and I peered out the window to see if I could catch sight of Tom or Huck, but I didn't spot neither of them. Maybe the newness of being in town got them curious, and they decided to take a look around. That seemed strange to me, though. Usually they didn't like to get too far away from Amos.

When Paris pulled up in front of Caraway's Dry Goods, there didn't appear to be anyone inside. Only one little light showed through the window.

"The store looks closed. You sure Parnell didn't go on to y'all's house?" I asked.

"No, I reckon he's in the back room. I suspect you better fetch that dog of yours before Parnell loses his patience with it. Tell Parnell I'm taking the car over to Lorelei's."

As soon as I slammed the car door behind me, Paris put her foot to the gas and roared off down King Street. All the sudden Huck was jumping all over me, like he'd been waiting forever for me to get there and rescue Tom.

"Down, boy," I told him, rubbing him about the ears. "You stay here while I go fetch Tom, and we'll get back to MeMaw's directly. Amos is probably wondering where you done gone."

The door to Caraway's Dry Goods was locked, so I pounded on it a couple of times to get Parnell's attention. He come out of the back room with a big grin on his face, like he were as happy as could be to see me, and unlocked the door. When he opened it to let me in, the bells hooked to the knob giving out a little tinkling sound, I could smell liquor on him.

"Well, hey there, Dovey. Nice of you to stop by for a visit," he said, motioning for me to come on in.

I looked about the store for Tom. "I didn't stop by for no visit, Parnell. I come to get Tom and take him home. What's all this about him biting you?"

Parnell walked over behind the counter. "Oh, he didn't bite me; just tried to, is all. I think maybe he done gone and got the rabies. He looked right demented."

"Tom ain't got no rabies. He's just got the good sense to know you ain't nothing but trouble," I told him. "Now give him over."

"Now why you got to go around talking about me that way, Dovey? I always been sweet to you." He moved over to the fountain. "Can I offer you something cold to drink? A soda, maybe? We got cherry and lemon, mighty tasty."

"No thanks, Parnell. I'd just as soon get Tom and leave, if it's all the same to you."

Parnell squirted cherry syrup and some soda into a glass and put it on the counter. "No, I can't say it is all the same to me, Dovey. I think it's time we made amends, don't you? Patch things up between us. Come on now and have you a glass of soda."

I walked over to the counter. "You ain't put poison in it, have you?" I asked as I picked up the glass.

Parnell laughed. "No, I ain't put poison in it. Look, I'll squirt me some, too." He filled another glass and took a sip from it. "See? Ain't a thing peculiar about this here cherry soda, no sir."

I picked up my glass and drank it down in one swallow. "Okay, Parnell, I done had a soda. Now let Tom out, and we'll be on our way."

"Can't do it, no, I'm afraid not," he said. "Not until we have us a little talk." He come out from behind the counter and stood next to me, the smell of liquor coming off his skin about to make me dizzy. "Dovey, Dovey," he said, turning to face me and shaking his head like he was real sad. "I've said it before and I'll say it again. It sure is a shame you didn't get your sister's good looks." He reached and touched a strand of my hair that had gotten loose from my braid. I backed away from him and said, "This ain't making me like you any better, Parnell."

"Oh, Dovey," he said, his voice as sweet as a mama talking to her baby. "I don't expect it matters what you like or dislike, not to anyone but you."

"What in damnation are you talking about?" I asked, moving farther away from him, a little trickle of fear starting to work its way through me.

Parnell got a real disappointed look on his face. "Now you know I don't like hearing that kind of talk out of you, Dovey. I reckon I'm going to have to punish you for that."

My insides turned cold listening to him, like a bitter wind blown through my skin. "Just give Tom over to me and let me go. That's all I'm asking." My voice shook a bit as the words come out.

"You ain't talking so smart now, are you?" Parnell smiled, then turned toward the back room. "C'mon, then, let's go see where Tom's at."

I followed him into a small, dark room lined with shelves. Metal soda canisters were stacked against the wall by the door, and a dozen or so twenty-pound bags of flour were piled next to them. It took a second for my eyes to get adjusted to the darkness, but when they did, I seen Tom in the corner of the room tied by a short length of rope to a pipe that run down the wall. He whimpered a bit when he seen me, his tail wagging, like he was ready to go home.

"I don't know why you got this dog tied up, Parnell," I said, turning around. "He wouldn't ever hurt anybody, not even someone as low-down as you."

Parnell bent to the floor and picked something up. Then he walked to the door. He was holding a brick in his hand. "Oh, this dog, it's a menace to society. Who knows what it might do to a little child."

"Why are you doing this, Parnell?" I asked, the words barely making it past my lips. My hand reached for the knife in my pocket. I pulled it out without Parnell noticing. My fingers was trembling, but I managed to flick the blade open with my thumb.

"I done told you, Miss Dovey Coe. I aim to teach you a lesson. You're always butting into other people's business, ain't you? And you're a regular mother hen to that brother of yours, watching over him like he was the younger and you were the older. But you can't protect Amos against everything, no sir. You can't have everything your way."

In a flash, Parnell drew back his arm and aimed that brick at Tom. That's when I stuck my knife out and made a wild stab at him. But it was too late. The brick left Parnell's hand and flew through the air. My blade tore through the sleeve of his shirt, a line of blood rising in a stain across the fabric.

Parnell bellowed and swirled around at me, his fist drawn back. As that fist come toward me, I slashed at him again. That's the last thing I remember.

When I come to, Huck was licking my face, and my head felt like it were split in half. I scooted myself so I was sitting up and rubbed my forehead, trying to stop the pain that was pounding against me like a hammer. It took me a minute to remember where I was. Tom lay in the corner, so stiff that I could tell he was dead. The tears filled my eyes, and I let them fall.

"How'd you get in here?" I asked Huck, who'd gone over and laid next to Tom, little whimpers coming out of his mouth. I looked about the room, wondering how long I'd been knocked out.

That's when I seen Parnell.

He was lying on the floor as stiff as Tom, one of them metal canisters a few feet from his head. I crawled over to him and passed my hand over his mouth. There weren't a breath left in him.

"Oh, Lord," I said out loud. "Oh, my Lord."

The bells tinkled on the front door, and a voice called out, "Parnell? Are you in here? I've been keeping supper on the stove for you for almost an hour."

It was Mrs. Lucy Caraway. She come to the door of the back room and reached in to flip on the light. That's when she saw us. "What in heaven's name?" she yelled, running over to Parnell. She put her ear to his mouth, and then felt his neck with her hand. "He's dead! Oh, my God! He's dead!" Then she turned to me. "You killed Parnell! You killed my son!"

chapter 13

They let me stay at home while I was waiting for my trial to come up. Usually when a person's been accused of a serious crime they make him stay in the jail lessen his kinfolks can come up with a right good sum of money. Bail, they call it. But the sheriff didn't figure I was likely to leave town before trial day, so he let Mama and Daddy sign a paper saying they'd be responsible for me showing up to court. The only thing was that I weren't allowed to cross the county line until after I was tried, and then only if I weren't found guilty.

They say it's at times like these when you find out who your real friends are, and by my reckoning the only real friend I had outside my family was Wilson Brown. Folks who'd always been right neighborly toward me, including them who were at Caroline's party, avoided my eyes when they seen me coming down the street. Not that I headed into town too much. I mostly stayed to home, helping Mama around the house and tracking through the woods with Amos.

Amos weren't himself after they brought Tom's body to him. It was like someone had cut off a piece of him and he weren't sure he could make do without it. It might sound funny to say it, but after Tom died, Amos got real quiet. Just at the time he said his first word, he stopped making any noise at all. Usually he played the rascal around the house, jumping out from behind doors to give Mama a fright or drawing funny pictures and slipping them into my books for me to find unexpected. But now mostly all he did was hike up into the mountain with Huck and come back empty-handed, like there weren't no use hunting things if Tom weren't around to hunt them, too. At home he'd sit on his bed rubbing Huck's head and staring out the window. I think he was hoping Tom might come running over the hill, him being dead just a bad dream.

Wilson come to visit me now and again, and he always made the effort to be right nice to Amos, patting him on the back and one time bringing him a real fine piece of quartz crystal from his collection. Wilson would ask Amos to join me and him on the porch, but Amos never felt much like it. So me and Wilson would sit by ourselves, eating the cookies MeMaw kept bringing up to the house to make everybody feel better and looking through comic books. We'd occasionally pass a few words between ourselves, but mostly we were quiet.

The only one who seemed his same old self was Daddy. After coming back from signing them papers at the sheriff's office, he sat me down at the kitchen table and looked me straight in the eye. "I hate to even ask, but I want to hear it directly from you so as not to ever have a single doubt. You ain't gone and killed Parnell, have you, Sister?"

"No, Daddy," I told him. "I didn't do it."

He nodded his head. "I didn't believe you had it in you. I hope you'll forgive me for asking."

He got up to go to work in the barn, but before he left he turned to me and asked, "You got any idea of who done it?"

"I ain't got the first idea, Daddy," I said. "When I come to, Parnell was laying there dead. I didn't see who done it."

"Could've been anyone, I reckon," Daddy replied before walking out the door.

That conversation seemed to settle things for Daddy. He was of the belief that if I didn't kill Parnell, then there weren't no way I'd be found guilty. He said he believed in the justice system and everything would turn out as it should. I weren't quite so sure.

We didn't have much money for a lawyer, so the judge assigned us one from all the way over in Wilkes County. Daddy insisted on putting down a little bit of money every week for his services, even though the judge said we didn't have to pay anything. Daddy wouldn't stand for that, though. As I've said, he weren't much for accepting charity.

The lawyer come up to see us a week before the trial to discuss what kind of case we had. Mr. Thomas G. Harding was a right handsome man about twenty-five or so. When he come up to the front porch after parking his car, Daddy greeted him at the door, saying, "You the lawyer's helper or something?"

"No, Mr. Coe," Mr. Thomas G. Harding replied, patting down the lapel of his gray suit. "I am, in fact, the lawyer himself."

"You don't look old enough to be no lawyer," Daddy said to him.

"I assure you, Mr. Coe, I am indeed a lawyer. I have a law degree from the University of North Carolina, the Chapel Hill campus."

Daddy ushered Mr. Harding into the house right quick. "Don't be saying that so loud. Folks around here don't trust city lawyers. The judge is likely to rule against Dovey on that fact alone."

Mr. Harding laughed, setting his brief-case on the kitchen table. "It will be our secret, Mr. Coe. Now where is Miss Dovey? Ah, this must be her." He walked over to where I was standing in the kitchen doorway and offered his hand to me. "It's a pleasure to meet you. Why don't we have a seat and talk about your case."

I sat at the table across from him, looking at the fine cut of his suit and his fancy haircut. "How come you're doing this?" I asked him.

"Doing what, Miss Dovey?"

"Taking on my case. From the looks of things, you don't appear to be the type to do much charity work."

Mr. Harding laughed again. He seemed a right jolly sort. "First of all, Miss Dovey, it's not charity work when it's paid for. And as for why I've taken your case, well, I feel it is part of my job to defend those who can't afford an expensive private attorney. In fact, that is one of the reasons I went into the law."

"To take care of poor folks?"

"Yes," Mr. Harding replied. "In a manner of speaking. I represent those who cannot afford representation. Liberty and justice for all, as I like to remind those with a tendency to forget that the laws of our country aren't only for the rich."

"You're a right learned fellow, ain't you?" I said. "They must pay you a sight of money for you to afford a suit like that."

"No, Miss Dovey," he said, opening his briefcase. "They don't pay me much at all. This suit comes courtesy of my father, who can afford closets full of such things. You certainly speak your mind, don't you?"

"She'll speak her mind till she's blue in the face," Daddy said from where he stood over by the sink.

Mr. Harding smiled. "Good, I like a person who's honest. Most people are too frightened to come right out and say what they're thinking."

"That's my belief, too," I told him. "Most folks are cowards when it comes to expressing their honest take on things. But that ain't how I am."

"Then we have something in common, Miss Dovey. I wouldn't be surprised to find we have many things in common."

We smiled at each other. I decided then and there that I liked Mr. Thomas G. Harding just fine.

We spent about an hour discussing the facts of what happened the night Parnell was murdered. I give him a little background on the situation, how me and

Parnell never got along, and how Parnell had spent all year being in love with Caroline, but she rejected him all the same. Mr. Harding took a whole mess of notes on a yellow writing tablet he brung with him. After I told him everything I known that could possibly affect my case, he leaned back in his chair and asked, "What do you think the other lawyer, the prosecutor, will claim motivated you to kill Parnell?"

"I didn't kill Parnell, I done told you that already," I said.

"Yes, Miss Dovey, you have told me that, and I believe you. However, the other attorney will say that you did, and he will create a story to show the reason you did. What do you think his story will be?"

I thought on that for a minute. "I reckon he might say that after Parnell killed Tom, I got so mad that I hit him over the head with that soda canister."

Mr. Harding nodded. "I imagine you're right, Miss Dovey. But let us continue to consider that matter as to leave no stone unturned. We want to be prepared for anything."

Mr. Harding stood up and began putting his papers back into his briefcase.

"She got a case there, Mr. Harding?" Daddy asked.

"I hope so, Mr. Coe. I certainly hope so."

Them weren't the most comforting words I ever heard, and I could tell Daddy weren't satisfied by them, neither. He walked Mr. Harding out to the porch and give him directions to the sheriff's office. Mr. Harding wanted to check on a few things with Sheriff Douglas before heading back to Wilkes County. When Daddy come back into the house, he patted me on the shoulder and said, "I suspect everything will work out, Sister. Don't you worry none." But there were plenty of worry in his words all the same.

The day of the trial we got up good and early to get dressed in a respectable fashion. Mr. Harding said it was important that I looked like I were on my way to Sunday school, so the judge and jury would think highly of me. I put on the yellow dress I worn to Caroline's party, and Mama combed my hair out real pretty so my bangs curled around my face. I looked like a right upstanding citizen by the time she was through with me.

"Dovey," she said to me when she was done with my hair, giving me a serious look. I was expecting her to lecture on me on how I was to behave in a ladylike fashion during my trial. Instead, she said, "I want you to remember that God takes care of his children. There's been a lot of praying done on your behalf, and I want you to take them prayers with you when you walk into that courthouse. Keep them in your mind if you start to worry that things ain't going your way."

"I will, Mama," I promised, and lay my head on her shoulder. She petted my hair a few times and give me a kiss on the cheek.

"Go on and get Amos," Mama said, rising. "I reckon we ought to go on now."

Amos's door was halfway closed. I nudged it with my foot, and it swung open to reveal Amos sitting with his back to me on his bed, writing furiously on a white sheet of paper. He must have sensed me in the room, because he turned around the second I took a step inside. He quickly folded up the piece of paper into a little square.

"This ain't no time to be writing letters, son," I told him. Amos shrugged his shoulders like he didn't have the least idea of what I was talking about. I followed him down to the truck, wondering what he was up to. Amos got in the way back with Huck, both of them looking scared.

The courthouse steps was already crowded with folks come to see the trial by the time we got there. Daddy's cousin Ray had driven Caroline over from Boone, and she run to greet us as soon as she seen the truck.

"How could they ever think you done such a thing as murder Parnell Caraway?" she cried into my ear, giving me a big hug.

Mr. Harding walked over then and shook Daddy's hand. He introduced himself to Caroline, but didn't give her a second glance after that. He was the first man I'd known who seemed to have more interest in me than in my sister.

Mr. Harding put his arm around my shoulder as we turned to go inside. "Are you ready, Miss Dovey?"

I told him I was, and all of us walked into the courthouse, except for Huck, of course. Amos tied him to a tree outside and gave him a bone to gnaw on. Usually Amos wouldn't bother tying Huck up, seeing as Huck's right afraid of strangers and won't mess with folks any. He'll run away from anyone he don't know, lessen of course they're on our property. Then Huck will go straight up to them and sniff them out to make sure they ain't up to any mischief.

But on that day, Amos wasn't taking any chances. I don't doubt he was thinking about what happened the last time Tom and Huck got away from him.

chapter 14

The prosecuting attorney, which is what they called the other side's lawyer, was a man by the name of Mr. Tobias Jarrell. I thought him to be a comical-looking sort, as he had no chin to speak of and his eyes was kind of buggy, like a frog's. But I had to admit that he was a smooth one. He could string words together and make them shine like lights around a Christmas tree.

"What we have here is an open-and-shut case, Your Honor," is how Mr. Jarrell started his argument against me on the morning my trial began. He said "Your Honor," but he was looking straight out at the folks lining the courtroom. You could tell he'd be real comfortable on the stage of a big-time theater, the way he paced back and forth as he spoke and took long, dramatic pauses. "As assistant district attorney of Watauga County, it is my job to present the facts and only the facts here in this honorable establishment. I am pleased to say that in this case, the facts speak for themselves."

"Then I suggest you let them begin speaking," Judge Lovett M. Young said. You could tell that he weren't the least bit impressed with Mr. Jarrell's theatrical talents. Because I was of such a young age, my fate would be decided by the judge alone, and I took comfort that the judge seemed to be a sensible sort.

"Very well, Your Honor." Mr. Jarrell made a little bow toward the judge's bench. "The facts that I will present to you here today are simple. A young woman enraged. A young woman with a knife. An upstanding, decent young man. Bitter words, bitter feelings. The young man cut down in his prime. The young woman, guilty of this heinous crime."

"Them Coes is trash," Paris Caraway said in a low, mean voice from across the aisle from where I was sitting.

"You best watch yourself, Paris Caraway," I said loud and clear as day to her. Mr. Harding, who was sitting in the chair to my right, took hold of my wrist and give me a stern look. "Miss Dovey," he said in a low, meaningful-sounding tone, "I must ask you not to respond to any comments made in this courtroom, no matter how much they might upset you."

I nodded like I understood, but I still saw

red every time I looked over to where Paris Caraway sat perched like a queen in her seat.

It was hard for me to look anywhere in that courtroom, except straight ahead. All the rows of benches was filled with folks who'd come to see the show, and I could feel their eyes upon me from the very minute I walked into the room, like I was some circus animal who'd escaped from the big tent.

Mama, Daddy, Caroline, and Amos was sitting in the bench directly behind the defense table, where me and Mr. Harding was seated. I couldn't bring myself to look at Caroline, her face was so full of misery and bad feelings, and I didn't want to look at Mama and Daddy, afraid that the sight of their faces might make me start crying.

I glanced at Amos from time to time, trying to figure out what he'd written on that sheet of paper. It filled me with nervousness to think about it. Every time I looked back at Amos, my insides got all jittery, and I had to remind myself to pay attention to the trial.

The first person Mr. Jarrell called up to the stand was Parnell Caraway's mama, Mrs. Lucy Caraway. I thought calling on Mrs. Lucy Caraway to be a witness weren't even fair, as she would of course have nothing but good things to say about her own son, and nothing but bad about me and my folks.

Mrs. Caraway carried a white handkerchief in her hand, and after she sat down and got sworn in by Deputy Coble, she dabbed it at her eyes every two seconds like she might never stop crying.

Mr. Jarrell come up to her, his face all sad and tore up, like he might start to cry, too. "Mrs. Caraway, it was you who found your deceased son's body, was it not?"

Mrs. Caraway sniffed into her handkerchief, then nodded.

"Please say your answer out loud so the court can hear you, Mrs. Caraway," Mr. Jarrell instructed her.

"Yes, I did," Mrs. Caraway replied in a soggy voice. "He was in the back room of my husband's store. And that wicked girl was standing right over him. Oh, she's the one who done it, all right. She killed my boy."

Mr. Jarrell nodded. "Did she say anything to you, Mrs. Caraway?"

"Oh, no, she just stood there, mute as that brother of hers. Didn't give a word of explanation."

"Mrs. Caraway, I know this is hard for

you." Mr. Jarrell moved in close and patted her hand. "But I'd like you to tell Judge Young about your deceased son, Parnell. What kind of man was he?"

"Parnell could be difficult, I admit," Mrs. Caraway said, and I almost fell over in my seat. I known a whole lot of folks who would have said the same about Parnell, but I never suspected his own mama would admit to it.

"Difficult?" Mr. Jarrell raised an eyebrow real dramatic-like. "How so?"

Mrs. Caraway sighed. "Oh, I don't know. I suspect we spoiled him some. He was such a smart, lively, cute little boy, it was hard not to. Eventually, he thought he should have the whole world placed in his lap." Then she looked up at Judge Young. "But nothing Parnell ever did earned him the punishment of being murdered. He weren't a bad boy, just strong-willed, wanting his own way."

Mr. Harding was nodding his head. "Smart. This is very smart," he whispered softly to me.

"What's smart about it?" I whispered back. What could be smart about bad-mouthing your own child, I wondered.

"Parnell *was* difficult," Mr. Harding said in a hushed voice. "The prosecution is saying it before we get a chance to. It will carry some weight with the judge."

I slumped in my seat. Their side was getting points for pointing out that Parnell was a scoundrel. That didn't seem fair to me.

"Mrs. Caraway, tell the court about this past summer, about Parnell's actions."

Mrs. Caraway blew her nose into her white handkerchief. "This summer, law. I don't know what was going on in that boy's mind, pursuing that Coe girl the way he did, always up there every spare minute of the day."

"Was this Miss Dovey Coe he was pursuing?" Mr. Jarrell asked.

"Good Lord!" I cried out. Mr. Harding shushed me, and Judge Young give me a hard look. But how could they expect me to stay quiet at such a question?

"Oh, no," Mrs. Caraway said, laughing a bit. "It was the older one, Caroline. She's a pretty girl, but that family, well, they're wild. Everybody knows that John Coe won't set foot in a house of the Lord. I suspect that's why that boy of theirs come out deaf. John Coe is a wicked man, and the Lord will punish the wicked." Mrs. Caraway coughed delicately into her handkerchief before continuing. "Oh, there are plenty of stories I could tell you about that family. I'll be surprised if only one of them ends up in jail."

Mr. Harding was up on his feet at that. "Objection, Your Honor! This is slanderous!"

"Objection sustained," Judge Lovett M. Young replied. That meant that he agreed with Mr. Harding.

Mr. Jarrell straightened his tie and cleared his throat. "Your Honor, I am merely trying to establish the circumstances of this summer, the environment that these horrible events were a consequence of. The defendant's family background, which is less than ideal, is relevant to this case."

Mr. Harding's hand was firm upon my arm. He known immediately that I was like to jump up over the table and box Mr. Jarrell's ears. Imagine that froggy-faced man saying such a thing! I tell you, I was on fire all over.

"Your Honor," Mr. Harding said, sounding like the whole matter was trying his patience. "Please! This is preposterous!"

Judge Young banged his gavel, which made Mrs. Caraway do a little hop in her seat. "Mr. Jarrell, I will allow you some latitude in your arguments here, given that family background can be an indicator of how a young person will be disposed to act. But you take care, sir, to back up with concrete and specific evidence any claims you make against the characters of these people. I will not allow rumor and innuendo in my courtroom!"

Mr. Jarrell made one of his little bows. "Certainly, Your Honor," he said, trying to sound humble. But I seen how his lips curled into a tiny smile, like he thought he'd won a victory here. He turned back to Mrs. Caraway. "Now, everyone knows, Mrs. Caraway, that you are not a woman to spread loose talk throughout the community. So, tell the court, if you will, what leads you to believe that the Coes have not provided a proper environment for their children."

"Why, everyone knows that John Coe likes the bottle." Mrs. Caraway had a prim expression upon her face. "I myself heard it from folks in my husband's store. I overheard someone talking to Johnny Hampton, saying that John Coe's corn liquor certainly had a bite to it."

"Objection, Your Honor! That testimony is hearsay, not to mention a complete fiction!" Mr. Harding called out.

"Objection sustained," Judge Young replied. He was starting to look like he could use him a rest from all the yammering going on, which I took as a good sign. I was getting tired of all these lies about my daddy myself. John Coe might not go to church, but that didn't mean he was some hillbilly with a still.

Mr. Jarrell cleared his throat again. "Mrs. Caraway, had you ever actually seen Mr. Coe take a drink?"

"I believe my son, Parnell, said he smelled liquor on John Coe's breath once when he was up to their place visiting."

"Your Honor," Mr. Harding said, throwing up his hands like all this was just too ridiculous to be believed.

Judge Young looked Mr. Jarrell straight in the eye. "You, sir, are to stop this line of questioning immediately. I told you I would not allow gossip and innuendo in my court, and yet that seems to be all that you're presenting here. I suggest you take a different line of attack immediately or I will cite you for contempt, sir!"

"Forgive me, Your Honor!" Mr. Jarrell said, sounding as sorry as he could be. "We'll move on to other things."

"Very well, then," Judge Young replied, then leaned back in his seat.

I give Mr. Harding a poke in his shoulder. "I reckon that Judge Young has taken a liking to us," I whispered, feeling the first bit of hope I'd felt all morning. "He seems to be on our side through and through."

"He's just doing his job, Miss Dovey," Mr. Harding whispered back. "We still have a long road ahead of us. Let us not lose sight of that."

Mr. Jarrell had turned back to Mrs. Caraway and surveyed her a bit, as though he was trying to figure out if it were worth his while to go on with her. Finally, he just shrugged his shoulders, looked to Mr. Harding, and said, "I'll turn this witness over to you, Counselor."

Mr. Harding stood up and hemmed and hawed a bit. I likened his actions to a batter swinging around his bat and kicking the dirt before going to the plate to hit a home run. Weren't no doubt in my mind that this trial was going our way. I leaned back in my seat, satisfied, hardly able to wait for Mr. Harding to grill old Mrs. Lucy Caraway over the coals about all them lies she'd been telling.

Mr. Harding made an odd croaking sound, and his face turned a bright red. Finally, rubbing his hand through his hair, he managed to get out, "The defense has no questions for this witness at this time, Your Honor."

And then he sat right back down.

chapter 15

I thought my head was going to blow off the top of my neck, I was so mad. "What is wrong with you, son?" I had to ask. "You act like this was your first trial, you're so flustered!"

Mr. Harding looked down at his papers, underlining words here and there with his fountain pen. His face was still blushing a furious red, but he acted like he was calm and collected. "It is my first trial, Miss Dovey. But that has nothing to do with my performance. I simply saw no reason to ask any more questions. Mrs. Caraway raised enough doubts by herself."

I didn't have time to say anything in response, as Mr. Jarrell had called up Paris Caraway to the stand. I would have to wait until lunch before letting Mr. Harding feel the full weight of my discontent.

I'll tell you one thing, Paris Caraway was a piece of work. I had known her since we was both real little, and she weren't what you would call an angel of a girl. But here, on this particular day, she looked as though she had the good Lord himself in her back pocket. Her dress was white with a hemline bordered in yellow embroidered daisies. It was the sort of dress Paris had not worn since she was eight and going to church on Easter Sunday, but the judge would not have been aware of that fact.

Paris settled herself into the witness stand and swore solemnly on the Holy Bible that she would tell nothing but the truth. I for one did not believe it, and as it turned out I was right to have my suspicions.

"Miss Caraway," Mr. Jarrell began, sounding like he was in the mood for a friendly conversation instead of talking to a witness in a murder trial. "Will you please tell the court about driving Miss Coe to your father's store so she could retrieve her dog on the night of August twenty-first?"

Paris looked to the jury and begun to speak in a real sad tone, like it were hard for her to talk about these things. I heard someone behind me murmur, "Poor child."

"Well, Parnell sent me up to Dovey's house, you see," Paris said, smoothing down the folds of her dress and picking at a thread, looking shy, "because he was worried about that dog of Amos Coe's biting somebody. It just seemed like that type of dog, if you know what I mean. Parnell got bit by a dog once when he was a little boy, and he remembered that fairly well enough."

Mr. Jarrell looked troubled, as though the thought of Parnell getting bit as a child disturbed his very soul. Then he stroked his chin, like he was pondering a serious matter. "What state was Miss Coe in when you found her at her house?"

"Jumpy," Paris answered, jumping about in her seat a bit to demonstrate. "She was sitting on her front porch steps polishing a knife. I was a bit scared walking up to the house, actually. Dovey seemed agitated to me. We'd been friends for many a year, and I'd never quite seen her in such a state."

"Can she just make lies up like that without no one saying a thing about it?" I whispered to Mr. Harding, who hushed me in response.

I wondered if it was too late to find me another lawyer.

"Please continue, Miss Caraway," Mr. Jarrell urged Paris.

"Well," Paris said, leaning forward, "I told Dovey she needed to come get that dog, and she was furious. 'Why do I got to do everything?' she wanted to know. And then she said something real strange, just as strange as it could be."

"What might that be, Miss Caraway?"

Paris lowered her voice a bit, like she were about to tell everyone the best secret they ever heard. I could feel the folks behind me straighten up in their seats, getting ready to listen. "She said, and I quote, 'If Parnell wants rid of that dog so bad, why don't he get Caroline to come get him?' Well, now, that didn't make sense to me at first. Everybody knew Caroline had left town already, and besides, what did that dog in my daddy's store have to do with Caroline? I was mystified."

She paused and looked around the courtroom, demonstrating her expression of mystification, eyes open wide, shoulders up in a shrug.

"But then I put two and two together. Dovey was upset about Parnell's proposal to Caroline. Why, Dovey was jealous. I probably ought to have explained to her right then and there that Parnell hadn't been serious about his proposal at all. He couldn't care a fig for Caroline Coe. But there was something about Dovey's agitated state that made me stay quiet. I didn't want to upset her."

I felt like someone had just hit me over the head with a rock the size of Tennessee, I was so stunned. If there was one thing Paris Caraway knew, it was how much the mere sight of her brother rankled me. And yet here she was, making up this fairy tale, lying with every bone she had in her body.

If my very freedom hadn't have been at stake, I would have laughed out loud at the foolishness of it all.

Mr. Harding was writing something on his yellow pad, seeming a bit agitated himself. I tilted my head to read his words. CRIME OF PASSION, they said in big, bold letters.

"I'm finding this all real hard to believe," I whispered to him. "The last reason I would have killed Parnell for was because I was in love with him, everybody knows that."

Mr. Harding simply nodded.

After pacing dramatically back and forth a few times in front of the witness stand, Mr. Jarrell made an abrupt stop and turned to Paris. "Miss Caraway, let me see if I am hearing you correctly. You believe Miss Dovey Coe was jealous of your brother's supposed affection for Caroline Coe?"

Paris nodded. "Yes, sir, I do."

Mr. Jarrell gave Paris a piercing look. "From most accounts, your brother and Miss Dovey Coe did not get along well at all. And you expect us to believe that, in fact, Dovey Coe had feelings for your brother?"

That was my question exactly. I was just a little surprised to hear the other side's lawyer asking it.

Paris shrugged her shoulders. "It came as a shock to me, too. But then I remembered something my mother told me. She said that sometimes the people who act like they hate you the most are the ones that love you the most. You know how the boys who throw rocks at you on the playground a lot of times would really like to kiss you? I think that that's how Dovey was about Parnell."

There was something about Paris's response that made me think this whole question-and-answer routine had been rehearsed just like a Shakespeare play. All the answers fit the questions just a little too easy, in my opinion.

"Miss Caraway, is there anything Dovey Coe said to you on your trip down the mountain to your father's store that makes you think she was of the mind to take some sort of revenge on your brother?"

"She was fairly quiet for most of the trip," Paris answered. "Though she did talk some of wanting to leave Indian Creek and how she might be doing that sooner rather than later. It made me sad to hear it, really. When I thought about it later, I guessed she planned on leaving town as soon as she murdered Parnell."

"Objection!" Mr. Harding called out, getting back into the swing of things at last. "This is the witness's opinion and has no place in her testimony."

"Objection sustained," the judge responded. It was the first good thing that had happened for our side in quite some time.

I had begun to feel as helpless as a baby. Paris could tell lie after lie, and there was nothing I could do to stop her. It was her word against mine, and it seemed like the judge would probably ship me off to the Home for Delinquent Girls in Charlotte before I even had a chance to tell my side of the story.

"I'm sorry, Your Honor," Paris said, looking down at her hands folded in her lap. "I didn't mean to speak out of turn."

"Just keep your testimony to the facts, young lady," Judge Young told her. He sounded like her kindly uncle, not the least bit mad.

"Yes, sir, Your Honor," Paris replied, giving the judge an oh-so-sweet smile.

Mr. Jarrell nodded to the folks in the courtroom, pleased that his star witness was acting such the lady in front of all them people, I suppose. Then he turned one last time to Paris. "Miss Caraway, did Dovey Coe say or do anything before she got out of the car that struck you as suspicious?"

I leaned back in my seat preparing myself for Paris's words, which I was sure would do me in for good. I could tell without even turning around that Paris had gotten everyone to her side of things, just by her being sweet and wearing a pretty dress. Paris Caraway could have run for mayor at that very moment and been elected, I dare say.

Paris twirled a piece of hair around her pointer finger and slowly shook her head. "Like I said, she'd been acting jumpy, but she didn't say anything at all suspicious at that point. I thought she was just upset about the dog and about Parnell's supposed affection for her sister," she said softly. "That's why it came as such a shock to me that they'd found her in the same room with Parnell. I didn't think Dovey had it in her to do such a thing."

There was no doubt in my mind at this point that Paris Caraway was killing me with kindness.

"Thank you, Miss Caraway," Mr. Jarrell said, his voice soft, too. "There are no further questions."

I looked to Mr. Harding, who had been writing long strings of sentences across his yellow pad all through Paris's testimony. He had to do something here, something that would crack open Paris's story like a knife prying open a walnut. I waited for him to rise up and be my hero.

But Mr. Harding just kept scribbling.

"Mr. Harding," Judge Young said finally. "Do you have any questions for this witness?"

Mr. Harding looked up, jerked out of his own thoughts. "Uh, no, Your Honor. She can be excused." Then he went back to his notes.

I heard a murmur of voices behind me. I didn't dare look at Mama or Daddy, for fear of the expressions they might be wearing. If I saw my mama's face crumble, I would mostly likely lay down on the floor and cry like a baby.

Mr. Jarrell called him one more witness before lunch, that being Sheriff Douglas. My mind was so full of worry that I barely paid attention to what the sheriff had to say about the evidence Mr. Jarrell was presenting — the metal canister found beside Parnell's body and my knife with Parnell's blood on it being the most significant things. Mr. Harding listened closely to every word the sheriff had to say, occasionally making a note or two.

After Mr. Jarrell finished questioning Sheriff Douglas, the judge said we was free to go to lunch for an hour but we was to return directly so that Mr. Harding could cross-examine the witness. "Should he care to do so," Judge Young added in a fairly sarcastic tone.

As soon as the judge dismissed us, Mr. Harding was gone in a flash, without so much as the briefest hint as to where he was off to. Mama tapped me on the shoulder and said, "Let's go have us a picnic, Dovey. It'll lift our spirits some after such a long morning."

I stood up and stretched my arms out, trying to push the worry from my bones. I heard low sobs coming from the other side of the room, and, like everyone else, I turned and peered to where the noise was coming from. On the end of the row, opposite of where my folks sat, there was Paris Caraway in her pretty white dress, her face buried deep in her hands, her mama petting her on the shoulder. I'd never seen Paris cry before, and it was a strange sight to me. Even stranger was that I believed her tears to be real.

Listening to Paris cry, I thought of how I

would feel if something so terrible ever happened to Amos. I let that feeling sink deep inside me, and when Mama took my hand to lead me outside, the tears were falling down my own cheeks.

For the first time since it happened, I felt terrible. It finally hit me that Parnell Caraway was really dead.

chapter 16

Mama led me out to the trees by the front of the courthouse, beneath which Caroline had unpacked a lunch of ham biscuits and sweet tea. I took a seat on the grass next to Daddy and leaned back my head to look up through the tree's branches. I thought I had best memorize the deep blue of the sky, the tree's knobby arms. After this trial was over, I might not have much chance to study on such things for a while.

When I sat up again, folks was streaming past us, making a point of not looking in our direction, with one or two exceptions. For example, when Curtis Shrew and Lonnie Matthews ambled by, they paused to have them a little laugh at my expense.

"Why, hey there, Dovey," Curtis called out. "You looking forward to being a flatlander? They're going to send you off to that girls detention home in Charlotte when this is all over and done with, that's for sure." Lonnie joined him in a big belly laugh at that remark.

"Why don't you boys move along now?" Daddy said, shifting a bit as though he was going to stand up and help them boys walk on if they didn't do so on their own.

"See you in twenty years, Dovey!" Lonnie called. Then he and Curtis walked across the street toward Caraway's.

"Don't listen to them boys none," Daddy said, giving my shoulder a squeeze. "Everything'll work out. That judge ain't sending you nowhere."

"It don't look good, Daddy," I said. "What's Judge Young supposed to think? There we were, me and Parnell and my knife. Ain't nobody else to lay Parnell's death on except me, now, is there?"

Daddy rubbed his eyes with his hands. He looked old all the sudden, and real tired. "Let's not talk about it right now, Sister," he said. "Let's just sit here and eat the lunch your mama made us."

Caroline passed me a ham biscuit. "Dovey," she said as I began to take me a bite, "I just want you to know that I realize this is all of my fault. I should have never taken up with Parnell. And I should have told him up front that I was still going away to school and wasn't interested in marriage. I embarrassed him so bad when he proposed, and then he went and took it out on you."

"This ain't no one's fault, Caroline," I said after a moment's quiet. "You had no way of knowing Parnell would be so vengeful. Most men would have just let it go."

Caroline began to cry silent tears, the way she always had, ever since she was little, never snuffling or sniffling in the least. I felt bad for her, but I couldn't help but think she was right, that if she'd just told Parnell flat out that she was going to college and wasn't ever going to marry him, we'd still be living our regular lives. But how could she have known her little games would end up with a man lying dead on a concrete floor?

After we finished with our lunches, Amos untied Huck and took him for a walk down to the creek that ran behind King Street. I started to go after him. I wanted to warn him not to do anything in that courtroom that would make us both sorry. But as I stood to follow him, Daddy took my hand and said, "You best stay here, Dovey. Someone might think you were trying to run off. We don't want nobody making a scene."

I sat back down, the knot in my stomach pulling tighter. I needed to talk to Amos, but I weren't going to get my chance, it appeared. I watched Mama and Caroline fuss with the napkins and waxed paper that the biscuits come wrapped in and then looked past them to the mountains that framed our town like a circle of wise old men and women. I noted Katie's Knob, one of the tallest and proudest among them, and I already missed running up her trail behind Amos, searching for all the interesting things a mountain had to offer.

Wilson Brown come up on me unexpected and sat by my side. "That Paris sure do like to make things up, don't she?" he asked.

I give him a nod in response, and Wilson fell silent. He was as good as Amos at picking up my moods, which made him a valuable friend. I wondered if the folks in Charlotte would let me write him letters.

Daddy started humming an old tune, "Sweet Molly Malone," I think it was, and you'd think it would have made me sad to hear it right then, but strange enough, it made me feel better.

I leaned back again, this time closing my eyes. It was time for me to think about this trial head-on. I needed to do something quick, especially if Amos was up to something, as I suspected he might be. Considering the matter at hand, Mrs. Caraway's testimony had helped our side, in my opinion, and Paris's testimony had harmed my chances, true enough. But what of Sheriff Douglas's testimony? Was there anything he had said that might be used to help my case?

I wished I had paid more attention when Sheriff Douglas had been on the stand, but I'd been too busy worrying about what Paris had said. I thought back as hard as I could. Mr. Jarrell had had the sheriff describe the scene of the crime, how he'd found Parnell's body and that of Tom's, how there'd been a cut on his arm and blood from that.

"Did the loss of blood from the cut kill Mr. Caraway?" Mr. Jarrell had asked the sheriff, and everyone had grown real quiet, waiting for the answer.

"Nope, it weren't the cut that killed him," the sheriff had answered, and you could hear everyone let their breath out again. "It was the blow to his head from that soda canister."

The canister had been sitting up on a table beside the witness stand, along with the knife and the shirt Parnell had been wearing, a small spot of blood on the sleeve from where I'd cut him. Mr. Jarrell had pointed to the metal canister and asked, "Is that there the murder weapon?" and the sheriff had nodded. "Yes, sir, it is. Like I said, the doctors say Parnell died from the blow to his head. That cut weren't deep at all, to tell you the truth."

Now that seemed to me a good point. Folks had spent far too much time talking about how I'd cut a man to death, but that weren't it at all. When I'd taken my knife to Parnell, it felt like it barely touched his skin. Most of the cut went into tearing that shirt.

I pictured that soda canister in my head again. It was about three feet high, with a round thing like a real small steering wheel atop it and a place where you attached the hose to let the soda run out. Who would have ever thought you could use such a thing to kill a man? Seemed odd to think about something as happy as an ice-cream soda or a cherry-lemon float being related to such a horrible act.

The last thing I had remembered that night in the back room of Caraway's was me stabbing at Parnell and tearing his sleeve and then him coming at me and my fall backward. What Mr. Jarrell needed to prove was that I'd gotten back up, taken hold of one of them soda canisters, raised it up high, and clobbered Parnell over the head with it.

How could he prove such a thing? I wondered. And then a worse thought came to me: Did Mr. Jarrell even have to prove such a thing? Was me being alone in the room with Parnell's body enough to get me convicted? It couldn't be that easy, could it?

It could have, but in a flash I had me a thought that made me burst out laughing. "I got it!" I yelled, startling Wilson and everyone else. "I know the answer!"

"What is it, Dovey?" Mama cried, coming toward me. "Are you okay? What is it that you got?"

I scrambled to my feet. "I ain't got time to talk to you now. But I reckon you'll see what I mean in a few minutes." With that, I ran toward the courthouse, aiming to hunt down Mr. Harding. I believed I had him a bit of information he could use to help us with our case.

The front hallway of the courthouse was dark and cool. I hurried down the long corridor, past the courtroom, where my very way of life was at stake, past the judge's chambers and the district attorney's office. I didn't rightly know where I was going, but I figured I'd be able to find Mr. Harding around here somewhere, as the courthouse seemed the natural habitat of a lawyer, even during the lunch hour.

All the doors was closed, and no lights shown behind them. I scurried down a flight of stairs at the hallway's end, my stomach all jittery and my blood racing through me like a train. The basement corridor smelled of mildew and cigar smoke. Once my eyes adjusted to the dim light, I saw just where that smoke was coming from. A cloud billowed from Sheriff Douglas's office, the door of which was open. From where I was, I could see Mr. Harding perched on the edge of the sheriff's desk, a fat cigar in his hand. As soon as he saw me, he stubbed it out. "Miss Dovey, I have some good news for you," he said, coming out into the hallway. "I've just had a very interesting conversation with the sheriff."

I smiled. "I bet it ain't as good as the news I got for you," I said. "It's going to bust this trial right open."

Mr. Harding looked at me for a moment, and then a big grin broke across his face. "Does your news have anything to do with a certain piece of evidence?"

I nodded. "It surely does," I said. I could barely contain myself and thought I might start jumping up and down from sheer excitement.

"You know, Miss Dovey, they say great minds think alike," Mr. Harding said, motioning me into the sheriff's office. "Why don't you come on in here and tell the sheriff what you're thinking?"

I walked straight into the sheriff's office. "I'd be glad to, Mr. Harding," I said, forgiving him all his earlier errors and poor performance. "Why, I'd be downright thrilled."

chapter 17

I had already taken my seat up front when my folks and Caroline and Amos come back into the courtroom after lunch. Mama and Daddy looked mystified, Caroline appeared confused, and Amos wore a nervous expression. I smiled at one and all as they took their seats behind me, then turned directly to Amos. "Don't say a word," I mouthed at him. "We got it all figured out." Then I turned around and waited for Mr. Harding to do his job.

After Judge Young called court back in session, me and Mr. Harding had to wait a long while to get to where we wanted to be. Mr. Harding declined to ask Sheriff Douglas any questions at that time, which seemed to make Judge Young a bit irate. In fact, I worried a bit that the judge might fire Mr. Harding for not doing his job and order me to get a new lawyer. Fortunately, the judge did not go that far. Mostly he just give Mr. Harding hard looks, which made Mr. Harding's face turn red each time, but he seemed prepared to stick things out until it was our turn.

To my surprise, Mr. Jarrell did not have many witnesses past Sheriff Douglas. He brought up Curtis Shrew to testify that I'd said I'd soon as shoot Parnell as look at him, which caused Mr. Harding to raise an eyebrow at me, but I simply shrugged my shoulders and said, "You know how I talk big sometimes."

Mr. Harding did not look pleased.

Finally, it was Mr. Harding's turn to present my case. The very first person he called to the witness stand was Sheriff Douglas, which made a lot of folks mumble and murmur. You could tell from the sounds of their voices they thought that Mr. Harding had had his chance with Sheriff Douglas and had let it go by. Mr. Harding paid the voices no attention, though. Everybody would understand soon enough.

"Sheriff Douglas," Mr. Harding started. "Would you please turn your attention to exhibit A and tell me what it is."

Sheriff Douglas looked over to the canister. "Well, sir, that's the murder weapon right there."

"Could you describe it, please?" Mr. Harding asked.

"That there's a metal soda canister. You

attach a little hose to it, and soda come out."

"I see," Mr. Harding said, like it was all news to him. "Now, Sheriff Douglas, would you describe the condition you found this canister in when you came across it at the murder scene."

"Well, it had a little dent in it from where it hit the victim on the head. And see that round thing on top?" He pointed to what looked like the thing you twist to turn on an outdoor spigot. "That had some blood on it."

Mr. Harding seemed to think this over for a minute.

"Was it Parnell's blood?" he asked finally.

"Ain't likely, sir," the sheriff answered. "Parnell didn't let no blood from his head. He died from what the blow did to the inside of his head, not the outside." He shrugged. "I reckon it belongs to whoever gone and killed Parnell."

"You had a chance to look at Miss Coe at the scene of the crime, did you not, Sheriff?"

"Yes, sir. I checked her for bruises and such, signs to see if she'd been struggling with Mr. Caraway."

"And did she have blood on her hands? Were either of her hands cut in any way?"

Sheriff Douglas answered immediately. "No, sir, I didn't see any cuts on her, but for the one on the back of her head."

"Could the blood from her head have gotten on that canister, Sheriff?"

"Not lessen she used her head to throw that canister at Parnell."

A few folks laughed at that. I turned around to Mama and Daddy, who both had smiles working around their mouths.

"Thank you, Sheriff, you've been very helpful. You may step down now."

A lot of folks commenced to talking as the sheriff made his way back to his seat. Judge Young pounded his gavel and yelled out, "Order!" Everyone quieted down right quick then.

Mr. Harding turned toward me. "I call Miss Dovey Coe for my next witness."

Another murmur went up, but Judge Young looked real threatening at folks, and that murmur went right back down.

"Miss Coe," Mr. Harding said in a right gentle voice once I had taken a seat on the witness stand. "Would you please describe what happened in the back room of Caraway's Dry Goods on the night of August twenty-first?"

I took in a deep breath and commenced speaking, wanting everyone to know exactly what happened once and for all. "Well, Parnell led me in there, saying he was going to fetch Tom, who was Amos's dog, but when I stepped inside the room, I seen Tom was tied up. Parnell said he was going to teach me a lesson, and when I looked at him he had a brick in his hand and was aiming to bash Tom's head in with it."

"What happened next, Miss Coe?" Mr. Harding's voice was full of concern, as though he were talking to me about a terrible and painful thing that had happened to me. Which, I reckon, it had been, even if I was still alive to tell the tale.

"Parnell was about to throw the brick at Tom, so I went after him with my knife. Then he come at me, and I cut into his shirt and caused him to bleed some. Then Parnell hit me across the face," I answered, remembering the fear that had filled me when Parnell had drawn back his hand. "I guess I must've hit the floor right hard, 'cause it knocked me out cold. When I come to, Parnell was laying there dead."

"So you're saying you didn't kill him?"

"No, sir," I replied in my most truthful voice. "I never did kill Parnell Caraway."

Mr. Harding turned to Judge Young. "Your Honor, if I may take the liberty of asking Miss Coe to step down from the witness stand to examine the evidence, I believe we may be able to clear up some things for you."

"Go ahead, Mr. Harding," Judge Young told him. "Just don't take all day."

"I promise I won't, Your Honor. Miss Coe, would you please come over and stand by exhibit A."

I walked to the table that the canister was set upon. All eyes were upon me, and I did my best not to shake from sheer nerves.

Mr. Harding lifted up the canister from the table, struggling to get a good grip on it, then set it down on the floor. "Miss Coe, would you do me the favor of picking up this canister?"

"Sure, I'm happy to oblige," I said, glad to finally show these folks a thing or two. Soon as I bent down and put my arms around that canister, the whole crowd understood exactly what Mr. Harding and me was up to. It must have weighed a good twenty-five pounds.

That soda canister was too heavy for the likes of me to pick up over my head.

Well, the room like to have burst with voices hitting against the walls once all them folks seen I weren't strong enough to lift that canister above my head, much less hit someone with it. Judge Young was pounding that gavel like he aimed to bust open his desk, but no one paid him no mind. I looked over to Mama and Daddy and seen the tears spilling from their eyes. Then I looked at Amos, who smiled at me before blowing a stream of air toward the ceiling, as though he'd been holding his breath during the whole trial.

Mr. Harding led me back to the witness stand. Folks quieted down then.

"I believe it's safe to say, Miss Coe, that you're not strong enough to pick up the canister that killed Parnell Caraway, is that correct?"

"I believe it's the safest bet around, Mr. Harding," I told him.

"Your Honor," Mr. Harding said, turning to Judge Young and bowing slightly, "I rest my case."

chapter 18

Winter come early to the mountains this year, delivering its first snow in the first week of November. Now the trees up on Katie's Knob stand dusted in white, and it looks like they got ghosts dancing through their branches. If you walk high enough up, you can see over the town, wood smoke curling up through chimneys and sending out the signal that folks are safe and warm inside their houses.

Most days when I come home from school, me and Amos grab a couple of gunnysacks from out in the barn and head up the mountain to collect mistletoe to sell to folks down in the flatlands. A man comes by on Saturdays to pay for it, and he takes it on to Winston-Salem and Raleigh, places that grown up so much, they ain't got much wilderness left to them. Huck comes with us when we go up collecting and sniffs around under logs and such, hunting for creatures that ain't burrowed in too deep for the winter. Now and again I catch him looking around like he lost something, and I imagine it's Tom he's wondering after.

Tom lays buried over to the barn, which is where we put him down when the sheriff brung his body to us, the day after Parnell was killed. Amos sits over by Tom's grave from time to time, making them signals with his hands he used to give for Tom to run and fetch something. I reckon when he does that, him and Tom are having a conversation about the old days up on Katie's Knob.

It was on a day when Mama sent me to the barn for a blanket to wrap around Amos as he sat by Tom's grave that I seen Parnell's ghost. It only happened that one time, but I suspect it will stay with me for the rest of my days. I was searching through the horse blankets Daddy kept piled in the corner, aiming to find one that weren't too dirty, when I sensed something was in the barn with me. I turned around and that's when I seen Parnell.

He looked like he always did, except I could see through him to the other side of the barn where Daddy kept his tools. It didn't scare me none to see him then, though later I trembled at the thought of it. "What are you doing here, Parnell?" I asked him.

He looked straight at me, his face full of

sad feeling. "Caroline," was all he said. Then he disappeared.

I never mentioned to anyone that I seen Parnell's ghost, but I think about it now and again. I remember how I felt that day in the courthouse, when I first realized that Parnell's being dead was a terrible thing. I still think it's awful sad, no matter that I never did like Parnell much and probably wouldn't if he was still alive today. But it makes a difference, knowing that his mama and sister loved him. It makes me think maybe there was more sides to Parnell than I known about.

They never did come to know for certain who killed Parnell. It took the judge all of thirty minutes to find me not guilty after Mr. Harding shown I weren't strong enough to have killed Parnell with that soda canister. Of course, a lot of folks still suspected me of doing it all the same, saying that it was possible I'd been so filled with passion and rage that I'd found within myself the strength to lift up the canister and knock it over Parnell's head, or that the cut from my knife was worse than Sheriff Douglas had said.

A couple weeks after my trial, a man's body was discovered on the banks of the Watauga River. Sheriff Douglas recognized him as someone who he'd thrown in jail a time or two for loitering around Indian Creek without no apparent business. He was from over in Ashe County, but when his folks come to collect his body to bury it, they said he'd been tramping around for years, getting in all kinds of trouble with the law, and only coming home every once in a while.

Turns out when Sheriff Douglas was identifying the man, he found a big cut on his right hand. That was reason enough for Judge Young to decide this man was mostly likely the one who done it, the one who killed Parnell. Judge Young closed the file on the case then, saying it was time folks got on with their lives and left the past behind.

I kept waiting for things to get back to how they used to be, but I started to be of the mind that things done shifted too far out of place for that to ever happen. On the surface of it, you might not have guessed that anything was different. Daddy still picked his guitar and sang his sad old songs, and Mama still wrote down our family history in her book. Caroline went on back to school and wrote us letters bragging on how well she was doing. Me and Amos still ran around on top of Katie's Knob searching out roots and whatever else proved interesting to us, but the feeling of all them things changed. It was like what happened with Parnell had touched us in a way that we couldn't shake.

From the beginning, I had my suspicions about who'd killed Parnell. It seemed right odd to me that Huck was in the store when I come to after Parnell knocked me on the ground. I known he'd been waiting outside for me, but if a stranger had come around, old Huck would have run off. He never took kindly to strangers, as I think I done told you already. The only way Huck would've come inside the store was if someone he known had opened the door.

The way I figured it happened is like this. After supper that night at MeMaw's, Amos come outside to sit with Tom and Huck and wait for me to come back from our house. Of course, Tom and Huck weren't there, so he figured they must have taken a notion to run around town to see what was about. When Amos come upon Huck waiting outside of Caraway's, he decided to look about inside to see if Tom had wandered in there. Maybe Huck had let him know somehow that's where Tom had gone.

He come inside the store, Huck on his heels, and started searching around for Tom. He didn't find him up front, so he headed for the back room, maybe thinking Tom had gotten into some food back there. What he seen then was Parnell standing over me, and me knocked out cold on the ground, maybe even dead. Staying real quiet, Amos searched around him, and his eyes landed on them metal soda canisters lining the wall by the door. He picked one up, Amos being strong enough to lift them things, and knocked Parnell over the head with it.

I guess once Amos realized he done killed Parnell, he got real scared and run off. I don't think he reckoned on me getting the blame for doing it. So he ran back to MeMaw's, where he bandaged up his hand from where he'd cut it lifting up the canister.

After the trial was over, I went to Amos's room to have a talk with him. He was sitting on the bed with Huck, staring out the window, when I come in. As soon as he looked at me, I could tell he known I'd figured it out.

I closed the door behind me and went over to sit next to Amos on the bed. "Amos, I ain't going to tell anyone what happened," I said to him. "And I don't want you telling, neither. If folks was to find out you done it, they'd say you was crazy and put you in a home for crazy people. You wouldn't ever come out again. You wouldn't ever see any of us again, and you wouldn't ever hike up Katie's Knob another time in your life. Do you understand what I'm saying?"

Amos nodded his head, the tears coming to his eyes.

"You never meant to kill no one — you need to remember that. It was an accident. Promise me you won't let no one know what happened. Do you promise, Amos?"

He nodded again, then buried his face in Huck's fur. I petted him on the back a few times, then went on back to my room, where I lay real still on my bed for the rest of the afternoon. That night after supper, I picked up my book to do some reading, and a note fell from it.

I thought he was going to kill you Dovey. It was the only thing I could do.

I took that note over to where we'd buried Tom that morning and scooped out some dirt from the grave. I buried Amos's note real deep, so no one would ever find it. As for that other note, the one he kept in his pocket during the trial, I suspect it was a confession, though I never did find out for sure. Amos was not the sort of boy to let others take the blame for what he had done, and that's what had scared me the most through my trial.

After I buried the note Amos left in my book, I went back inside and washed my hands. Looking at my face in the mirror over the sink, it come to me all the sudden that Amos had probably saved my life. Who knows what Parnell would have done if Amos hadn't come in when he did. All these years I'd been watching over Amos like he couldn't take care of himself, and in the end he was the one who took care of me. I swallowed hard when that thought come to me. I known then it was time for me to admit that Amos didn't need me to be his protector anymore. It was time for me to admit that I'd always needed Amos as much as he'd needed me.

I only ever told one other person about what happened, though I had my suspicions that Mama known. After Sheriff Douglas testified that there was blood on the soda canister, I seen Mama take a long, hard look at Amos's hand where he still had a little scar on it from his cut. She never said a thing about it, though, and I heard her telling MeMaw a few weeks later that she was glad Parnell's killer had shown up in the shape of that man they found drowned in the river.

Mr. Harding come over to the house for supper a few days after they found me not guilty. He claimed he was up to file some paperwork, but I figured he'd gotten fond of Mama's cooking and was looking for an opportunity to eat a good meal. When Mama announced supper would be ready in twenty minutes, I asked Mr. Harding if he'd like to take a walk with me up to Katie's Knob. He said that sounded like a fine idea.

"You know, Miss Dovey, I've always wanted to apologize for my poor performance at the beginning of your trial," Mr. Harding said as we started out on the path. "I wasn't very effective, I admit."

"You found your way soon enough," I pointed out to him.

"In the nick of time, you mean." Mr. Harding slapped his palm against his forehead. "You know, I'd spent hours pondering that evidence before the trial started. Why it didn't come to me before that the canister had to be too heavy for you to lift, I have no idea."

I shrugged. "It didn't come to me any earlier, either," I told him. "I ain't no lawyer, but usually I got some common sense."

Mr. Harding nodded. We walked on in silence for a few moments, enjoying the cool scent of the woods in winter.

"Well, Miss Dovey, you are a free woman," Mr. Harding said at last. "How does that feel to you?"

"It feels mighty fine, Mr. Harding, mighty fine, indeed," I replied. Then I brought up what I'd been wanting to ask him ever since the trial was over. "I was wondering, though, are you still my lawyer?"

Mr. Harding give me a curious look, then said, "Why, yes, Miss Dovey, I am. I still have papers to file over at the county courthouse, and until the time I do so, I remain humbly in your service."

I hugged myself against the cool breeze coming off the mountain. "I been reading me some law books over at the library, and they say anything I tell you, you can't tell anyone else. That true?"

"It certainly is, Miss Dovey. Whatever you say to me, I am bound by law, not to mention honor, to keep confidential. Is there something you wish to share with me?"

That's when I told him all I had figured out. After I got done explaining the whole story to him, I asked, "Is there any way someone could point the finger at Amos and get him sent away for killing Parnell?"

Mr. Harding thought this over for a moment. "I would think if anyone suspected Amos, that person would have spoken up by now. Moreover, Judge Young has closed the file on the case and is quite unlikely to reopen it. I think we have nothing to worry about, Miss Dovey. I believe Amos has every chance for a free and prosperous life."

I smiled at him then. All us Coes was excited about the news Caroline had brung with her from teachers college. She had found a book in the library that showed how to do a special sign language for deaf people, and that got her to thinking. She spoke with one of them professors of hers, telling him about how smart Amos was and how he loved to read books and write things down. This professor told her that when Amos got older, he could learn how to be a teacher of deaf children using them hand signs in the book. She brought that book home for Amos, and he set down to studying it right away. He was real pleased with the idea of being a teacher.

We reached the top of Katie's Knob and could see Indian Creek spread out below us, the streets all aglow in the last light of day. I pointed out the various places to Mr. Harding: the courthouse, Pastor Bean's church, Caraway's Dry Goods, the places I had known all my life.

As we were walking back to the house for supper, I said real casual to Mr. Harding, "You reckon you'll be asking Caroline out for a date?" Frankly, I'd been real curious as to why Mr. Harding didn't seem to be under Caroline's spell. I'd finally gotten to where I didn't blame Caroline for anything anymore, and I'd decided it was all right if Mr. Harding decided to fall in love with her. I'd enjoy having him around Indian Creek, to be honest.

Mr. Harding give me a look like he didn't know what I was talking about, then laughed. "Ah, Miss Dovey, are you trying to play matchmaker? Well, I suppose I should have mentioned that I have a lady friend in Wilkes County with whom I have an understanding. Besides, Caroline is not half as fascinating as her sister is. Miss Dovey, you are a mighty big force to be reckoned with."

" 'A mighty big force to be reckoned with'? Why, Mr. Harding, you talk like you was one of us Coes!" I laughed.

"Nothing would please me more than to be one of you Coes, Miss Dovey," Mr. Harding said, sounding serious.

I took his hand in mine and thrown him a big grin. "Shoot, Mr. Harding, the way I see it, you already are."

We walked hand in hand back to the

house, where supper waited on the table. How does it feel to be a free woman? I asked myself as we walked through the door. The answer come back to me right simple.

It felt better than anything I had ever known.